D1058105

SHERLOCK HOLMES
and the
Mysterious Friend
of
OSCAR WILDE

SHERLOCK HOLMES
and the
Mysterious Friend
of
OSCAR WILDE

RUSSELL BROWN

Based on and Incorporating Writings
of Sir Arthur Conan Doyle
and Oscar Wilde

ST. MARTIN'S PRESS • NEW YORK

Design by Judith A. Stagnitto.

Library of Congress Cataloging-in-Publication Data

Brown, Russell A.
   Sherlock Holmes and the mysterious friend of Oscar Wilde / Russell
A. Brown.
       p.   cm.
   ISBN 0-312-02280-8
   1. Wilde, Oscar, 1854–1900, in fiction, drama, poetry, etc.
   I. Title.
   PS3552.R7145S5   1988
813'.54—dc19   88-16890
                                                    CIP

First Edition

10 9 8 7 6 5 4 3 2 1

To A.C.D. and O.F.O.F.W.W.

It was your lives and writings which first suggested the idea of this little tale to my mind.

For this, and for the help which you gave me in its evolution, all thanks.

Yours most truly,
Russell Brown

'Circumstantial evidence is a very tricky thing. It may seem to point very straight to one thing, but if you shift your point of view a little, you may find it pointing in an equally uncompromising manner to something entirely different.'

Sherlock Holmes

'To give an accurate description of what has never occurred is not merely the proper occupation of the historian, but the inalienable privilege of the man of arts . . .'

Oscar Wilde

'The . . . artist is known by the use he makes of what he annexes, and he annexes everything.'

Oscar Wilde

'I have never been nervous about details, and one must be masterful sometimes.'

Sir Arthur Conan Doyle

Contents

Foreword   xi

Acknowledgments   xv

1. Unnatural Intrusions   1

2. Protecting the Family—A Humbled
    Holmes   19

3. Result of a Fruitless Inquiry   36

4. An Ignoble Surprise   41

5. Strange Virtue and Ominous Advice   62

6. A Family Circle: Misery, Violence,
    Fear   65

7. A Private Invitation   75

8. Doings in the Street   78

9. A Fortunate Hansom   85

10. Wilde Revelations   91

11. Dragging the Net   112

12. The Tale of a Ghostly Hound   121

13. Weir, Not a Mews   141

14. Leaving the Friends Behind   144

15. Coming Together   148

Appendix   168

Foreword

*I*n the spring of 1988, workers converting a London town house found a concealed safe, which they proceeded to open with nitroglycerine. Inside was a manuscript signed "John H. Watson, M.D." and a letter signed "Sherlock Holmes." No proof of authenticity was found, but some facts are known:

For the first forty years of this century the house was owned by Sir Frederick Mackintosh, an immensely successful solicitor and friend of many prominent persons including King Edward VIII (in whose abdication Sir Frederick played a crucial, though unpublicized, part, earning himself a knighthood). Thanks to the ease with which he was able to move among all levels of British society between the end of Victoria's reign and World War II, Sir Frederick proved adept at conciliating disputes that might have embarrassed society if allowed to reach the courts. His greatest disappointment was his failure to prevent Winston Churchill from suing for libel Lord

Alfred Douglas, former companion to Oscar Wilde; his proudest accomplishment, establishment of a refuge for homeless boys in London.

Little is known of Sir Frederick's private life, except that he was a confirmed bachelor whose youthful life-style was characterized by E. F. Benson as "unconventional" but whose later years were devoted to preserving the British ideal of home and family. He died during the Blitz, from a direct hit on a Turkish bath. Ironically, it was the one where he had first met Dr. John Watson, shortly after Sherlock Holmes had retired and retreated to Sussex Downs. (There was much speculation about this separation, until Dr. Watson explained, during the surprise testimonial dinner tendered by the Detective Police Force, that although he was a Hampshireman born and bred, he preferred to endure the irritations of London rather than "wallow in the bucolic charms of a Sussex farm." A different explanation is suggested in the "Sherlock Holmes" letter published here as an Appendix.)

Except for a brief resumption of practice (as a prison doctor), Dr. Watson lived in retirement his last twenty-five years with Sir Frederick, chronicling more of Sherlock Holmes's adventures and pursuing a philanthropic activity. He died in April 1928 from a chronic heart ailment.

There is a strong tendency, whenever a new Sherlock Holmes story appears, to regard it as genuine. The public's insatiable demand has fostered a cottage industry supplying new stories, two of which come quickly to mind: *The Seven-Per-Cent Solution* and the inaccurately titled *Last Sherlock Holmes Story*. One recalls George Bernard Shaw's remark: "As far as I can ascertain, I am the only person in London who cannot sit down and write an Oscar Wilde play at will. The fact that his plays, though apparently lucrative, remain unique in these circumstances, says much for the self-denial of our scribes." One wishes that

Sherlock Holmes's admirers would exercise the same denial. For this reason, we regard this story skeptically.

In its favor are the letter (whose signature, compared with that of the latest offered for sale at Sotheby's, appears genuine) and the revelations of this eminent Victorian couple's personal relationship. To its disadvantage (besides the nature of that portrait, which may offend some) are two facts: One-sixth of the manuscript is identical to passages in the published works of Dr. Watson and Oscar Wilde, and the chronology of some events differs slightly from historical records. (This circumstantial evidence is not, of course, conclusive, as both authors were known to repeat themselves, and Dr. Watson was not above bending chronology to make a good story seem even better.)

If the story is not genuine, speculation centers on Sir Frederick, an amateur author who amused himself by writing stories about a raffish thief. But this raises a greater mystery: Why would he devote enormous time to pasting together other authors' words, connected with his own narrative? Was it a finger exercise for his own writing, or was there a more subtle purpose, perhaps suggested by Sir Frederick's favorite quotation, Oscar Wilde's advice to aspiring authors: "Produce the modern idea under an antique form."

To withhold the story until the truth be known would do the public a disservice. Accordingly, we are presenting it now with no warranty, inviting readers to judge for themselves—on internal evidence or their own inclinations—whether to accept or reject its startling revelations.

THE EDITOR

Acknowledgments

*L*ike Oscar, I have a high regard for the Family. The constant support of mine made this book possible. Love and gratitude to Frederick and Margaret, Barbara, Ellen, Laura, Ernest III, Eric, and Ernest II.

Regina and Charles Reynolds, Ronnie Dane and Alvin Rabinowitz provided criticism and encouragement.

Michigan librarians in Vassar, Bay City, Saginaw, Midland, and Caro provided research materials.

Michael Denneny was the First Cause and, for years, indefatigable advocate. Without him there would be no book.

I would also like to thank Donna Rossler and Julie Lasky at St. Martin's for their work on the manuscript.

Books by four generations of writers (most of them "late") provided insights, and background. Among the best: W.H. Auden, E.F. Benson, John Dickson Carr, Rupert Croft-Cooke, Lord Alfred Douglas, Richard Ellman, St. John Ervine, Andre Gide, Nicholas Halasz,

ACKNOWLEDGMENTS

Michael and Mollie Hardwick, Michael Harrison, Sir Rupert Hart-Davis, Charles Higham, H. Montgomery Hyde, Jerome K. Lawrence, Pierre Nordon, Hesketh Pearson, Henrik Schück, Edgar W. Smith, Ragnar Sohlman, and Vincent Starrett.

Above all others, *The Annotated Sherlock Holmes* was a continuous inspiration. To its editor, the late William S. Baring-Gould: Ave! but never vale.

CHAPTER ONE

Unnatural Intrusions

Q ueer people sought help from Sherlock Holmes, but the queerest of all arrived one morning in the spring of 1895.

Almost a year had passed since my return to Baker Street after a five-year absence, which had begun with my marriage and had continued through the three years of Holmes's disappearance and supposed death over the Reichenbach Fall, an event followed hard upon by the death of my wife.

Plunged into grief again, I had gravitated back to Baker Street, where Mrs Hudson and I exchanged memories and pored over her scrap-books of articles published at the time of Holmes's death. I blush with shame to recall how I patronised her simple-minded faith that one day Holmes would stride back into our lives, as he did on April 5, 1894, with such suddenness that, for the first time in my life, I fainted. Shortly afterwards, at his invitation, I sold my practice and returned to Baker Street.

It had been naïf of me to expect that Holmes would return the same man, but one thing that had not changed was the intimate relationship between us. I was still his closest friend, partly due to Holmes's aversion to women and disinclination to form new friendships, but also due to my own qualities. 'A confederate who foresees your conclusions and course of action is always dangerous,' he confessed to me, 'but one to whom each development comes as a perpetual surprise is, indeed, an ideal comrade.'

As for me, I was stimulated by this man who had brought into my life such excitement and adventure, allowing me to share with him and to chronicle the social and official scandals of the late Victorian era, and although at forty-three I was two years older than he, I never forgot that my whole purpose in life, indeed, my greatest joy, consisted in serving him.

Holmes's solution of the mysterious death of Ronald Adair had initiated a period of prodigious activity involving scores of unsolved cases. His energies were taxed to the limit, but his relish at being back in London, at the centre of five millions of people, cheered me, for I knew that nothing stimulated him more than activity, and nothing exhausted him more than idleness. Then, the single weakness of his nature would come to the fore, and the alert, active man give way to the pallid dreamer of drug-created dreams.

The day before our queer visitor's arrival had been dreary and trying. Confined to the flat by drizzly fog, Holmes had prowled restlessly about, glancing frequently towards his morocco case, with its deadly contents. Seeking to distract him, I had drawn forth Mrs Hudson's scrapbooks, but his only response was, 'One never knows what others think of us until we are dead.' Finally, I had shown him *The Strand* magazine, with 'The Final Problem', my account of his death, hoping that this time his usual indifference to my attempts would be supplanted by some genuine appreciation. Alas, he only chuckled, drew from the bookcase a slim blue volume, marked a passage, and dropped it before me. I declined the bait, and with a shrug of indifference he departed the flat.

When I arose the next day, I felt no sense of refreshment, the Jezail bullet which I had brought back in one of my limbs throbbing with dull persistency. I huddled on my clothes and hastened down to our sitting room. I am naturally Bohemian in habits myself, but the sight which met my eyes filled me with indignation. From wall to wall the carpet was littered with cigarette ends and crumpled newspapers. Had each been a dead soldier, I might have imagined myself surveying the melancholy scene following the Battle of Maiwand, where I had acquired my injury.

'This time he's gone too far!' I exclaimed to Mrs Hudson, who bustled in with my breakfast cover, her round, ruddy face full of its morning cheeriness. Ignoring my outburst, she launched into an account of the morning's events, which instantly usurped my attention.

A telegram had knocked her up at dawn. She had brought it to our sitting room, only to find 'Mr Holmes! In woman's costume!' (I was not surprised, knowing that Holmes had, in different parts of London, five refuges where he changed his personality, and that he often took advantage of the freedom allowed by feminine attire.) Hardly had Mrs Hudson retired to the lower hallway than Holmes had come bounding down the stairs, his face 'as black as thunder, and with an answer for the boy that— well, I'm a respectable woman, and I never heard such an answer!' Then, Holmes had apparently distracted himself by combing all the journals before retiring.

'I do wish Mr Holmes would rise. I'm going to Mrs Turner's to watch her children while she visits her husband in hospital. He's the constable who was blown up yesterday at Scotland Yard by the Dynamiters. He was in the loo and *whooom*! Can you imagine, setting it off *there*? That's not playing the game! Socialists, Anarchists, Red Republicans—why do they want to *change* things? There's never been a better time than 1895, and there never will be.' She picked up the book that Holmes had marked. 'Plato. Would that be a cook-book?' Before I could reply, she pointed to my nitroglycerine tablets. 'I do wish you wouldn't keep those in my house.'

'Nonsense. I need them for my heart trouble. If my dear wife—'

'Bless her soul, if it hadn't been for her passing, you wouldn't have come back to Baker Street. There's good and bad in everything, and you can't separate them any more than you can the ingredients in a good soup, once you've put them in. And if you could, well, your soup wouldn't be worth eating!' She frowned at Holmes's morocco case. '*That* isn't medicine. It makes Mr Holmes sick. Mr Holmes! Would you care to take breakfast?'

Holmes's bedroom door had opened, and the man himself appeared, wearing his mouse-coloured dressing-gown and an irritated frown. Without a glance at either of us, he strode to the mantel and filled his pipe from the Persian slipper. 'Black coffee, rashers and eggs, and a quiet room to eat them in.' Mrs Hudson fled the room, and Holmes turned to face me. Even in a dressing-gown he was a formidable figure, in height over six feet, and so lean that he seemed to be taller. His eyes were sharp and piercing, and his thin, hawk-like nose gave his whole expression an air of alertness and decision.

'Well, Watson, you've made a fine mess of this room.' Holmes picked up one of the journals. 'Another attempt by the Dynamiters upon the Nelson Monument—unsuccessful, or I should have had to credit them with improving Trafalgar Square.' He placed the journal neatly upon the foot-stool and picked up another. 'Item: Further comments upon the death of an industrial aristocrat. It's a mercy we can't read our own obituaries.'

'*You* did.'

'A touch, I do confess. What have we in the apocrypha of the agony-column? Item: "We are not deceived. Expect you to fulfill bargain. Wait for further instructions".'

'Arrant nonsense, that agony-column bleat.'

'This would make sense if we knew the vital clue: What is the mysterious "bargain"? Item: A languid paragraph by Langdale Pike' (Holmes's erstwhile friend and human book of reference upon all matters of social scandal and gossip of the metropolis). ' "Friends of a prominent detective are concerned about his obvious tendencies. Only a miracle can prevent a scandal." Hopkins? Lestrade? But they aren't "prominent".'

'I don't care about Pike's peculiar obsession with other people's affairs.'

'I shouldn't care, either, if I had anything else to occupy my mind. "How weary, stale, flat, and unprofitable seem to me all the uses of this world", to quote a Melancholy Scandinavian. There is nothing new to do; it has all been done before.'

Mrs Hudson bustled in with Holmes's breakfast tray.

'Please send Billy to Bradley's for a pound of their strongest shag,' commanded Holmes. (He was incapable of remembering children's names, and had long since solved the problem by calling all of our page-boys Billy and all the leaders of his auxiliary force Wiggins.)

'He's not here!' wailed Mrs Hudson. 'Something terrible must have happened. I have a feeling, and I always trust my feelings before I trust my head.'

'I shouldn't expect the worst,' Holmes dismissed her. He indicated *The Strand*. 'By the by, Watson, I see you could not resist exaggerating the dramatic elements of my death.'

'No more than could you the dramatic elements of your return. I am ashamed at my fainting like a woman.'

'You know my weakness: Some element of the artist wells up within me and calls insistently for a well-staged performance. But while I exterminate this egg, be so good as to read aloud the last two lines of your chronicle.'

' "Such was the end of him whom I shall ever regard as the best and the wisest man I have ever known",' I provided from memory.

'Highly flattering, though somewhat derivative.' I have been told that my face reveals every emotion, and it must have proclaimed incredulity, for Holmes added, 'Make a long arm to Plato's *Death of Socrates*, which you ignored yesterday, and read out the marked passage.'

' "Such was the end of my friend, whom I may truly call—" ' my voice faltered at the dreadful similarity ' "—the wisest, the justest, and the best of all the men whom I have known".' Holmes's grey eyes were dancing with amusement and triumph. 'I shall have to change it in the next edition,' I concluded lamely.

Holmes was relentless. 'Which? "The Final Problem" or *The Death of Socrates*?' He jabbed a fork towards my pill-box. 'Those nitroglycerine tablets have intimations of mortality. There's a good chap, remove them.'

'Perhaps you will dispose of your morocco case. What is it now?'

'Cocaine. A seven-per-cent solution.'

'Metred suicide. And it's only a matter of time before clients notice those puncture marks on your wrists.'

'My mind is like a racing engine, tearing itself to pieces because it is not connected with the work for which it was built.'

'Why don't *you* catch those Dynamiters?' demanded Mrs Hudson, returning to gather up the dishes.

'Doctors reveal themselves by a nitrate of silver stain on the right forefinger; dynamiters do not advertise their profession, or we should have to suspect Watson.'

'We should do what Her Majesty wants: make a law against selling dynamite. You can't change human nature, but you can always change the law. And if they can't buy it, they can't blow it up! Lord bless me, I nearly forgot there's a person downstairs to see you.'

'How interesting,' replied Holmes with deceptive casualness. 'A male person or a female?'

Mrs Hudson reflected. 'It could be either—or it could be both.'

'And what does this person of indeterminate sex look like?'

'Look like?' She paused dramatically. 'Like a giant moth.' She threw her arms akimbo and fluttered them in such comic impersonation that Holmes and I burst into laughter. 'His name is Mr Oscar Wilde.'

'Confounded insolence!' The smile withered on Holmes's face and he leapt to his feet. 'I sent word that I would not see him.'

'I'm happy to hear you say it, sir,' said Mrs Hudson, marching to the door.

Holmes's violent response intrigued me. 'Do you know him?' I enquired.

'I know *of* him, and of his notorious father.' Holmes seized from the bookshelf a red-covered volume. Leafing quickly to a page he read: ' "Sir William Wilde, surgeon, founder of famous hospital for eye and ear diseases, lecturer on travel and scientific curiosities, decorated by King of Sweden. Three children, one named Oscar after King Oscar of Sweden." Burke's *Peerage* tells only bare facts.' He dropped the red book and snatched up a bilious, pale-green one. 'Langdale Pike's *Golden Treasury of Victorian Scandals* includes the trial resulting from Sir William Wilde's alleged violation of a woman patient under anaesthesia. His wife testified she was "uninterested" in the fact that he had fathered illegitimate offspring. She had herself previously figured in a trial, as writer for the Young Independence Party.'

'Their son—?'

'According to Pike, Oscar Wilde is High Priest of the Decadents, leader of a band of London aesthetes who comprise a cabalistic society as unhealthy as ours is healthy. Things repulsive and unnatural to us are, to them, mere commonplaces of existence.'

It would be idle of me to say that I was unfamiliar with this sort of thing. I had encountered it in school: the classmate whose face came aglow with unholy light when the rugby master described ancient Greek athletes competing naked; the history master who took pains to mention certain tendencies of Edward II, James I, and William III; the classics master who stressed the sexual proclivities of Sir Francis Bacon and Christopher Marlowe, and even hinted at Shakespeare himself. In medical school professors labelled it criminal pathology, but a student ventured opinion that punishment of such transgressors (until recently, in England, by death) was a vestige of those dark ages when the mentally ill were whipped to expel demons. In time, he suggested, we might view these men as sufferers from an insufficiency disease.

I could not agree. I believe my mother was closer to the truth when she told my older brother that carnal desires are wicked and can be controlled by resolution. (I grieve to think how poorly it served my unhappy brother who, turning to drink and a life of guilt-ridden sensuality, pursued an adventuress to San Francisco, where I nursed him through a loathsome disease, performing terrible offices.)

'In recent years,' Holmes's voice drew my thoughts back, 'their members have increased. In '85 an Amendment to the Criminal Law established severe penalties, but in '89 a scandal occurred at a house in Cleveland Street, where men and boys came together.'

As Holmes spoke, feelings of revulsion rose within me. I opened my lips to speak, but—'My dear Mr Holmes,' came a strange voice from the doorway. Holmes and I spun about to see Mrs Hudson standing by the door, apparently having lingered. Behind her loomed a grotesque figure.

It looked, indeed, like a giant moth, in black frockcoat, light-coloured trousers, brightly-flowered waistcoat, white silk cravat with pearl pin, pale lavender gloves and lavender spats, lucent top-hat, and carnation buttonhole. Beneath hair cut in the style of Nero loomed a smiling, yellow face, stout, puffy, coarse-grained, and greasy, with heavy double chin and pendulous lip—only redeemed from grossness by two extraordinarily bright eyes which gave a startling impression of youth. The apparition before us—tall, massive, with a suggestion of uncouth physical inertia, and holding a lily—could only be the notorious Oscar Wilde.

'My dear Mr Holmes,' he repeated, lumbering in with a jerky, zig-zag gait more elephantine than moth-like, 'you will excuse me for not remaining below, but the hallway wallpaper is so ghastly; one of us had to go.'

'What are you doing with my lily!' cried Mrs Hudson.

'It looked so lonely. If I'm ever reborn, I should like to return as a flower. Perhaps a red geranium—for my sins.'

'Or a green carnation,' said Holmes coldly, his lips a thin line.

'How baroque,' replied Wilde, holding out the lily.

Holmes's face was granite. 'My interest in flowers is limited to opium, poisons, and belladonna—in all of which useful properties the lily is deplorably deficient.'

'Pity. I think it is better to take pleasure in a flower than to pursue indiscreet revelations of its life underground.' He proffered the lily to Mrs Hudson, who flounced from the room. I expected that Wilde would notice he was unwelcome, but he began removing his gloves. 'I have read so much about you that I feel like an insubstantial character in fiction next to your palpable reality.' He extended his hand. Holmes plunged his to the bottom of his pockets. Wilde turned to me and clasped my hand with his flabby and greasy flipper. 'How good to see you again, my dear Dr Watson.' My face must have been a study in scarlet; Holmes's proclaimed astonishment and then an unpleasant, dark suspicion. Somewhere in my mind stirred a vagrant memory. Where had I met him? 'The American publisher's dinner,' he prompted, 'five years ago when we were both beginning writers. Your conversation was scintillating.'

'Scintillating!' Holmes's voice taunted. 'I never get your limits, Watson. There are unexplored depths to you.'

'It is easy to scintillate when infatuated with one's subject. You are fortunate in your Boswell, Mr Holmes; it is usually Judas who writes the biography.' I freed my hand from his grasp. 'Dr Watson is clearly one of those who without possessing genius have a remarkable power of stimulating it.' Despite his grotesque appearance, the ingratiating manner almost seduced me. 'The story he wrote, *The Sign of Four*, deserved far more attention. Did either of you read mine, *The Picture of Dorian Gray*?'

'"A poisonous book, heavy with mephitic odours of moral and spiritual putrefication, for exiled noblemen and perverted telegraph boys",' was the astonishing reply from Holmes, an omnivorous reader with a strangely retentive memory for trifles.

'You read the notices! Praise makes me humble, but when I am abused I know I've touched the stars. We live in a time when only the dull are taken seriously, and I live in terror of not being misunderstood. But surely you know more than that about my works.'

'I know they contain the epigrammatically-expressed opposite of everything a true Englishman holds dear.'

'I have as much respect for the Englishman's beliefs as you have for the criminals you pursue. They are our Loyal Opposition: Without them, we would both be out of occupation. The cleverly-expressed opposite of any popularly-held belief has an irresistable fascination for the Press—a most valuable institution, if you only know how to use it. Thanks to them, I cannot walk down Piccadilly without hearing people say, "There goes that bloody fool, Oscar Wilde." It's extraordinary how quickly one gets known.'

'That is not fame. It is notoriety.'

'It is not what you do in this life that counts, Mr Holmes, but what you can make people think you do.'

'I have said the same thing,' said Holmes coldly.

'In *A Study in Scarlet*. The moment I read it I thought, "I wish I had said that." Now I have.' Wilde appraised our room. 'La Vie Bohème!' He picked up Burke's *Peerage*. 'The best thing in fiction the English have ever done.' He glanced at the woman's costume, and in a voice filled with insinuation he exclaimed, 'Ah!' He passed to my portrait of General Gordon.

'A great man!' I hastily remarked.

'No, but a great *poster*.' He shambled towards Holmes's chemical table. 'The only thing I know about chemicals is that alcohol, taken in sufficient quantities, produces all the effects of intoxication.' He held up a strip of blue paper. 'May I ask—?'

'An infallible test for blood stains. The litmus paper tells.'

'How clever of it.' My head whirled. I felt as if I were watching Holmes at the scene of a crime picking out details which enabled him to form conclusions about the persons who inhabited or passed through it. 'Now, we must get down to business,' said Wilde briskly, seating himself. 'My dear Holmes—you don't mind my calling you Holmes, and you shall call me Oscar.'

'You will kindly give me my prefix when addressing me. And as no state of affection exists between us, I insist that you cease calling me your "dear".'

Wilde smiled. 'It is inappropriate to a client relationship.'

'You are no client of mine.'

'No, my friend is.'

'I have no interest in your friend, as I said in my reply to your telegram, which I assume you read.'

Wilde beamed at Holmes in the most infuriatingly charming manner. 'If I had, I shouldn't be here, should I? Do you have a cigarette?' He opened Holmes's morocco case, exposing a hypodermic needle and vials labelled *Cocaine*. Holmes smoothly, but a trifle tardily, dropped the sleeve of his dressing-gown over his wrist. Wilde closed the case. 'A cigarette is a perfect type of a perfect pleasure. It is exquisite and it leaves one unsatisfied. What more could one want?' Holmes made as if to rise. Wilde quickly added, 'The case is blackmail.' Holmes relapsed into his chair. 'I have heard that in delicate matters you are most discreet.'

'I have heard that you cannot be blackmailed.'

'From whom have you heard about me?' asked Wilde.

'An impeccable source: a blackmailer himself. From whom have you heard about me?'

'A despicable source: the Marquess of Queensberry. You gathered evidence for your friend Lady Queensberry's divorce suit.'

'If ever a woman was wronged by a brute of a husband it was she.'

'The court proceedings took all of fifteen minutes. But the Scarlet Marquess learned of your good offices, and he has placed you before Christianity in the Pantheon of his favourite hatreds. He has told my friend, "I have Sherlock Holmes to thank for a good deal—and I shall pay the debt".'

'The old sweet song. How often have I heard it.'

'Do not think that indiscretion is any part of valour. The Marquess is so dangerous that, if he were not a noble lord, he would long ago have been confined to a madhouse. He has repelled friends of his own class, alienated his children, and lavished on Lady Queensberry every fiendish ingenuity of cruelty and meanness, inundating her with vile letters. It is his only connexion with literature.'

Holmes disdained the warning with a curt, 'Thank you for the advice.'

'Friends can be chosen at random, but one can never be too careful in the choice of one's enemies. But to the case: I have so much experience with practitioners of blackmail that I have acquired a reputation amongst those who share my passions and fashions of life.' An expression of disgust came over Holmes's face. How, I wondered, could Wilde ever hope to gain my friend's assistance? 'On this curious mixture of romance and finance I have become an unofficial consultant—the only one in the world.'

'I am a busy man,' interrupted Holmes with more force than truth. 'Kindly come to the point.'

'Mr Holmes, I consider blackmail to be the most

despicable of crimes, destroying or holding in bondage a man's character, that immortal part whose loss may be a fate worse than death.' Holmes had expressed the same sentiments to me. No circumstances could be more likely to excite his curiosity. 'A mutual friend recognized his anguish and directed him to me. I have come to beg assistance, though I am not at liberty to reveal names.'

Holmes rose to re-charge his pipe. 'Your client is noble.' The effect upon Wilde was extraordinary. His facial muscles tensed, his pendulous jaws quivered, his purple lips struggled silently. Finally, he replied, 'In saying that, you are not far out. I have many noble friends, including one at Buckingham Palace.' Holmes nervously clasped and unclasped his hands upon the stem of his pipe. What luck for Wilde, striking the chords to which Holmes's every fibre vibrated. Blackmail! Royalty! We were as good as off on the hunt already.

'There can be no question of public credit,' added Wilde, 'but the financial rewards may be considerable.'

'My concern is neither money nor credit.'

'I understand. Art for Art's Sake.' Wilde glowed with satisfaction at the consummate skill with which he had wrought such a change in Holmes, and I could scarcely help admiring it myself. Then, with victory in his grasp, he made a fatal error. 'And I shall take pleasure in working with you.'

Instantly, Holmes reverted to his distant manner. 'It sounds not only sordid but trivial. I must decline to involve myself.' There was resounding silence in the room, broken only by the faint clanging of the doorbell downstairs. Wilde's smooth, assured manner gave way to a faltering question: 'You dismiss the case?'

'I dismiss *you*. If we should meet in public, kindly do not acknowledge our acquaintance.'

In the distance the doorbell pealed again. Wilde lurched to his feet. 'I am disappointed in you, Mr Holmes.'

'It is only your approval that could in any way annoy me. You will excuse me if I do not rise to see you out.'

Wilde drew himself up. 'Rudeness is like a rare wine. I am honoured that you have reserved for me your finest vintage.' He bowed and lumbered towards the door. Passing the table, he paused at sight of the blue book. '*The Death of Socrates*. I recall the case: corrupting the young.'

'Mr Holmes! Lord bless and save us! Help!' From the lower hallway came the voice of a woman in violent hysterics. Holmes and I leapt to our feet, but before we could move, rapid feet clattered upon the stairway, there was a tumultuous rush in the hall, the door burst open, and Billy, our missing boy in buttons, plunged into the room, pursued by Mrs Hudson's voice, 'Oh, my poor lamb!' An instant later she waddled in, followed by an alert, eager young man in unofficial tweeds.

Wilde was first to regain his composure. 'I feel a superfluous figure in this drama.' Casting an appraising eye upon the young man, who stared back in astonishment, he lurched out the door.

'Save me, sir!' cried Billy, his hands in manacles.

'Hopkins, what the deuce is the meaning of this?'

'He's under arrest!' interposed Mrs Hudson.

I looked with sympathy at the young man, Inspector Stanley Hopkins, whom Holmes regarded with favour as one of the most promising young detectives at Scotland Yard. His handsome young face was suffused with embarrassment. 'Mr—Mr Holmes,' he stammered, 'I—I had no idea—Mrs Hudson—'

'Explain yourself.'

'I will, sir, if Mrs Hudson will leave the room.'

'With my little lamb in custody? Not if I hope to see salvation!'

'Perhaps, Hopkins, you could speak obliquely.'

'I was on duty, sir, at the head of Charles Second Street, and Master Billy came out of a private residence.'

'I should like to see you arrest *me* for that,' interrupted Mrs Hudson.

Hopkins's words seemed wrung out by main force. 'It's a *house*, sir—' he concluded in a whisper '—like a house in Cleveland Street.'

There was silence of the sort I remembered from the war, when an explosion died away, leaving tortured air. Then: 'Cleveland Street!' bawled Mrs Hudson. 'Oh, Lord have mercy upon us!'

'Silence!' Holmes's voice cracked. 'This is no place for a woman.'

'No place for a woman!' Mrs Hudson wrapped her arms about the trembling boy, her eyes blazing with unaccustomed fire. 'I sha'n't be put out of my place by anyone—begging your pardon most respectfully, sir.'

'There've been complaints about this private house,' Hopkins resumed. 'People coming and going. Men and working-class boys. Scotland Yard's had its eyes upon it for some time, but someone must be protecting it. Of course, if some noble lord should complain—but you know how it is, sir: one law for the poor and one for the rich.'

Holmes's voice was stern. 'I hope you're not turning Socialist, Hopkins.'

'Oh, no, sir. I'll always stand up for the way things are, however I may think of them.' Hopkins lowered his voice. 'I was afraid someone would recognise him as your page. He's not a bad lad, sir; I just put the derbies on to make sure he'd never go back.'

'You are the best of the Professionals, Hopkins,' said Holmes, bestowing praise which he usually reserved for Inspector Lestrade. 'Billy!' I have never seen Holmes look more like an avenging angel. The boy came forward like a whipped puppy.

'I've lost my character, sir, haven't I?' He fell sobbing at Holmes's feet. 'Please don't send me away, sir! I would die if I had to leave you.'

'My little lamb,' said Mrs Hudson, 'you won't have to leave us, not while Martha Hudson has breath in her body.'

'You have done a wicked thing,' said Holmes in his most magisterial manner, 'but I shall allow you to redeem your character.' The boy attempted to kiss Holmes's hand. I looked away in embarrassment (and to hide my own tears). 'Mrs Hudson, wash Master Billy's face. Then bring him back so he can go for shag.'

As the door closed, the three of us scarcely dared look at each other. Then: 'It is a national disgrace!' Holmes's words crackled. 'Compared to this place, a house of ill-repute is respectable; at least the crimes committed there are natural. But these crimes strike at the foundation of national life—the Family—and we have a duty to protect the children of respectable parents from the unnatural lust of full-grown men.'

'But the boy wasn't harmed—' Hopkins seemed curiously unstirred.

'Wasn't harmed!' Holmes's reply made him cringe. 'He'll bear scars the remainder of his life. There may be no way to close this house legally, but I've a mind to go there and thrash these miscreants.'

'Very dangerous!' warned Hopkins. 'The house is under surveillance.'

'Damn the surveillance! Damn the danger! And damn these men!' Holmes strode to the stick rack and snatched down his favourite.

'Good show, Holmes!' I cried, seizing the loaded hunting-crop.

'Mrs Hudson,' Holmes told the bewildered woman, who had reappeared in the doorway, 'we are going to Charles Second Street to teach these villains that London is not a City of the Plain.'

'But—but sir—' Hopkins stammered frantically, 'there's a better way.' I was losing patience with Hopkins. There was something unmanly about his attitude. 'The man who was here, sir—'

'A villain, despite his effete bon mots. There are no fools so troublesome as those who have some wit.'

'He has a reputation for liking boys. Those at Charles Second Street are small fish, but—'

Good man, Hopkins, I thought, my faith in him returning. 'After all, Holmes,' I added, 'you haven't any cases in hand now.'

'True. I think we shall pay a call first upon Mr Wilde.'

'Will you come, Hopkins?' I asked.

'Being in the Force, it wouldn't be proper.'

'*I'*m not in the Force!' cried Mrs Hudson, clambering upon the sofa and snatching a whip from the rack in such a menacing manner that I pitied any man who came within its reach.

'This is no work for a woman,' said Holmes. 'Come along, Billy. We'll show you how to deal with men like Mr *Oth*car Wilde.'

I hastened after Holmes and Billy, down the steps to the street, leaving Mrs Hudson hopping up and down upon the sofa, brandishing her whip and cheering: 'Go it, Mr Holmes! Go it, Dr Watson! Treat 'em proper for my little lamb!'

CHAPTER TWO

Protecting the Family—
A Humbled Holmes

*O*ur cab ride from Baker Street to Wilde's residence was grim, Holmes sitting upright and silent, Billy huddling in the corner. As we turned into Tite Street and drew up at a four-storey residence, there emerged from the front door a grave little Artemis with great curls of chestnut hair.

'Wasn't she beautiful, Holmes?' I remarked as he paid the cab.

'Who?'

'Really, you are quite unobservant about some things.'

'You know I am not a whole-hearted admirer of women, Watson. They are never to be trusted, even the best of them.'

We were admitted to the house by a pompous butler who informed us that Mr. Wilde had just returned, and, after enquiring within, invited us to wait in the writing room. It was a model of neatness and restraint, with a bookcase, a few chairs, and a writing table. The only decorations were an attractive painting (which I had seen somewhere before) and, on a pedestal in the corner, a Greek-type statuette of a naked man, which I quickly turned to the wall before Billy could observe it. 'Bad enough in museums,' I remarked, just as Wilde entered and greeted us like old friends.

'Mr Holmes! How good of you to return my call so promptly.' He extended his hand, and again Holmes ignored it. 'Constance, my wife, has just left. She will be so disappointed; she is a great admirer of yours.' Holmes, I knew, was accessible on the side of flattery, but Wilde's attempt was fruitless. 'You seem surprised not to find me in an Arabian Nights drawing room, like Thaddeus Sholto's in *The Sign of Four*. (He's a relation of my friend, Lord Alfred Douglas.) The Bourguereau (I winced as he pronounced it) was Sholto's. A typical mixture of bad art and good intentions; it is really all done by hand.' He turned me about to face the table in the bow window. 'My desk belonged to Carlyle.'

I had long admired my Scot countryman, whose aphorism about genius and pains had inspired me to pursue excellence. Wilde was undeniably ingratiating, as I remembered his being at the dinner, where he had towered above us all, yet seemed to be interested in all that we could say. Had I judged him only by his charm, I would have considered him the most pleasant person I had ever met.

'I suppose, Mr Holmes, you have come to accept the case.'

'I accept only that you are a blackguard.'

'A small agreement, but at least a beginning. You share that judgement with most of London and all of the Press. May I ask why you are maundering about London with such anachronous accessories?' He indicated Holmes's stick: 'A Penang lawyer, used in the tropics upon lower castes. And my dear Dr Watson, the last riding-whip I saw was in the hands of the Marquess of Queensberry on fox-hunt: the unspeakable in full pursuit of the uneatable.'

'We are not here to indulge in trivial banter!' I reproved him.

'My dear Dr Watson, I believe we should treat all the trivial things of life seriously and all the serious things with sincere and studied triviality.'

'That is not the attitude of this young man, who has suffered at the hands of your ilk!'

'Indeed. What is your name, young man?' enquired Wilde of Billy.

The boy, obviously repelled by Wilde, retreated behind Holmes and replied in an almost inaudible voice, 'Billy, sir.'

'You believe his misfortune concerns me,' said Wilde, touching a bell.

'We are here,' I replied, 'to protect the children of respectable parents from the unnatural lust of full-grown men—and to protect the Family!'

'My dear Dr Watson and Mr Holmes,' said Wilde, 'although I permitted you to treat me rudely in your scandalous Bohemian abode, I do not allow anyone to speak to me that way in my house, the residence of a family gentleman. If you have come here to abuse me verbally, I am more than a match, as can be attested by many who have crossed swords with me—once. If you intend to assault me physically, I warn you: At University I studied the manly art of boxing—Queensberry rules—in preparation for dealing with those who prove their manhood by bullying, and who believe that I am their natural prey. I did not allow the Mad Marquess and his professional bruisers to bully me here, and I shall not allow you.'

The door opened to admit a keen-faced boy of about ten years. I stared appalled. I have known men who displayed beautiful women as evidence of their manly conquest, but I never imagined that one of Wilde's kind would dare to flaunt his catamite. I rose to leave, as Wilde said, 'This is my son, Cyril.' Addressing the boy in the kindest manner, he said, 'Do you remember the stories we read in *The Strand*? I have a surprise for you. This is Mr Sherlock Holmes and Dr Watson.'

'I am very happy to make your acquaintance, sir,' said the boy, making a pretty bow to Holmes and extending his hand. Holmes, who held opinion that hand-shaking was an adult amenity, declined to accept it. 'And yours, sir,' said the lad, making another bow to me. 'You are a very good writer.' I could not forbear shaking his hand. 'But if my father had written the stories, they would have been funnier.'

Wilde laughed indulgently. 'That is the trouble with praise; it is so often tainted with criticism. Cyril has wondered, Dr Watson, whether your wife, after *The Sign of Four*, lived a long and happy life.'

'My dear wife did live happily, but I grieve to say not for long.'

'I am sorry. In literature the bad are always punished and the good rewarded with long life. I suppose that is why it is called fiction.'

'May I go now, Father?' asked the boy. 'Cook is making pastry.'

'Not even Mr Holmes can compete with pastry. Yes, but save some for your brother. Perhaps you could share with Billy, while Mr Holmes and I converse.' Remembering the selfish child-fellows of my youth (and perhaps myself) I would not have given tuppence for Billy's chances. To my surprise Cyril answered:

'Of course, Father, if you like.'

At mention of pastry, Billy's shyness fled. 'May I, Mr Holmes?'

Cyril bowed to each of us again, then planted a kiss on his father's cheek. 'Thank you for calling me, Father.' As the door closed behind the boys, I felt sympathy for Holmes. He strongly believed, and had demonstrated to me in 'The Copper Beeches,' that by watching the behaviour of a child one might gain a valuable insight into the character of its parents. This healthy, gentle, polite child had certainly disproved the theory.

'A find lad, most polite manners,' I remarked.

Wilde glowed. 'I am very proud of him, and of his brother. You will understand, if you ever have children yourselves. May I offer you a seat, Mr Holmes? Though I prefer you remain standing. Height is the chief beauty of a man. It gives presence.' To my surprise, Holmes sat. 'We were speaking of Protecting the Family. I have a high regard for the Family; I *came* from a Family. My father is deceased, but I still maintain a close relationship with my brother—who is often on alcoholiday—and with my mother, for whom I have always felt the greatest love and honour. I exist because my Family had different tendencies from mine; I love them because of and despite that, and I hope they will always accord me the same consideration. In addition, I *founded* a family. I have a wife and two splendid children who are all the world to me. I respect their tendencies as part of their individualism, and because the happier they are in theirs the less likely they may be to resent mine.' Gazing into my face, Wilde concluded: 'How could anyone imagine that I do not value the Family? It would be as if I did not value the bank which holds my savings, upon which I depend for my entire existence.'

I was keenly aware that the man's smooth-flowing argument was flawed by sophistries, but I found it difficult to put my hands upon them. 'It is still the foundation of national life!'

Holmes, who was impatient with less alert intelligences, had once remarked that he knew exactly how a battery feels when it pours electricity into a non-conductor. Wilde now exhibited the same impatience. 'When you look at the Family, you see it as the Peaceful English Home, an oasis of tranquility surrounded by a howling desert of crime. When I look at it, all I can think of is the impunity with which crimes can be committed *within* it, crimes which are, in the Family, mere commonplaces of existence. If we could hover over this great city, gently remove its roofs, and peep in at the things which are going on in each Family, we would realise that the vilest alleys in London do not present a more dreadful record of crime than does the dear old English home. There is no lane so vile that the scream of a battered woman or the cry of a tortured child does not beget instant indignation among the passers-by and set going the machinery of justice. But look at those Families, each in its own cloister. Think of the deeds of hellish cruelty, the hidden wickedness which may go on, year in and year out, within each one, and none the wiser. To suggest that *these* Families are the foundation of national life is itself a crime, a sacrilege, a villainy. The foundation of national life is not the Family—it is the *happy* Family.'

'And we must protect it!'

'"Protect the Family." A blood-stirring battle-cry. But what the Family most needs protection from is itself, and we may best protect it by ensuring that our own does not comprise a group of strangers, unwillingly bound together, for purpose of mutual destruction. Has anyone ever told you, Mr Holmes, you listen with your eyes?'

'Has anyone ever told you, Mr Wilde, you are as subtle as the serpent in abstract argument?'

'Then I shall descend from the general to the particular. You know the circumstances of Lady Queensberry's life with the Mad Marquess. Can you conceive of the harm done to her and to her children by his contempt for them? No one is more self-righteous than he in decrying threats to his Family; no one threatens it more than he.'

It was obvious that so long as Wilde spoke upon this subject he would have us at disadvantage, but I knew his vulnerable point. 'You don't like women!'

'My dear Dr Watson,' he replied in tones of sweet reason, 'I adore women. I would be guilty of your charge only if "liking" meant feeling compelled to pursue, harry, nuzzle, woo, and impregnate every woman who comes within my view. But if "liking" women means valuing them as individuals and appreciating their sensitive qualities, I am an enthusiastic admirer. I cannot understand men who claim to admire women, but who repress any womanly qualities in themselves. There is nothing I admire that I do not want to make a part of myself, and if I didn't want to, I should feel hypocritical to claim that I value it. Surely, Dr Watson, *you* understand. With your athletic physique and conspicuously hearty manner you appear never to have heard of such things as books. But you could not write as you do without having a high degree of feminine sensitivity.'

'I beg your pardon, sir!'

'Do I understand, Mr Holmes, that you have never married? Pity. Every experience is of value, and marriage is certainly an experience.'

'I have too much appreciation for the solitary life—'

'There is nothing like marriage to increase your appreciation for the solitary life.'

'—and a woman would try to reform me.'

'Women love us for our defects. If we have enough of them, they will forgive us everything, even our intellects.

Of course, to you a woman would be a continual irritation: They are all clues with no solutions. Remember that, should you ever be tempted to enter into a more conventional relationship with the opposite sex—as have I.'

'I see no reason for prolonging this interview,' said Holmes, rising.

'Wasn't it curiosity about these things that brought you here, along with a suspicion that I might be of help in clearing Billy's character?' Holmes's answer was to pick up his hat and stick. 'I am sorry you will not accept my help, but perhaps some friend of yours who is "so"—'

'I have no friends of your ilk.'

'You do, and it is only because you are unaware of them that you find it so easy to be contemptuous. I am sorry that they are forced to hide their deepest natures from you.'

'My ramifications stretch into many sections of society, but not into those which you seem to regard as peculiarly your kingdom,' said Holmes.

'Another regret. You will be at great disadvantage, prowling through a world of whose dangers you are ignorant.'

'No one knows the criminal world of London better than I!' said Holmes, bristling.

'I see,' replied Wilde, 'you do not rank modesty among the virtues. But mine is not the criminal world, only a different one, unknown and quite impenetrable to you.' Holmes's hand touched the doorknob, and Wilde hastily added, 'I am bored. There is nothing new to write; it has all been written before. I propose a friendly competition: I shall look into Billy's case, and you will look into my mysterious friend's. I'll wager I can resolve one mystery before you can the other.'

'You'll lose that wager!' I cried, incited by the instinct which drove me to spend half my pension on the turf.

'Your self-assurance exceeds the bounds of arrogance,' said Holmes.

'Beat me, Mr Holmes! Humble me to your will!'

'You are a cunning tempter.'

'The only way to resist temptation is to yield to it.'

'I have had to do with fifty murderers, but the worst never gave me the repulsion I feel for those who practise your unnatural vice.'

'We have no need to practise; we are already masters of our trade. And there is nothing so commonplace as what you call "unnatural". Remember: "One's ideas must be as broad as nature if they are to interpret nature".'

'See here!' I admonished. 'Holmes said that in *A Study in Scarlet.*'

'The Devil can quote scripture for his purpose,' said Holmes.

'And so can the self-righteous, when they want to condemn the sins they have no mind to. Everyone is so willing to make others good; I call it the Depth of Morality.'

'I warn you: I fight the Devil every day and I win.'

'I fight the Devil every day and I never win. I suppose that's why I have a more serene temperament than you.'

'I will not bandy words about your beliefs!'

For the first time, anger flashed in Wilde's eyes. 'I believe in personal liberty for every human soul. I believe each ought to do what he likes and develop as he will. What do *you* believe in, Mr Holmes? You doubtless consider me selfish to live as I want to live. But true selfishness is asking *others* to live as you wish to live. To be truly unselfish is to let others' lives alone.'

'I don't agree with a word you've said,' replied Holmes, 'and I don't think you do, either.'

'I assure you, I almost do.'

'Strange rumours about your wickedness have become the scandal of the clubs.'

'I love scandals about other people, but scandals about myself don't interest me: They haven't got the charm of novelty. As for wickedness, it is nothing but a myth invented by good people to account for the curious attractiveness of others.'

'You ignore the dictates of modern morality!' I expostulated.

'I never came across anyone in whom the moral sense was dominant who was not heartless, cruel, vindictive, log-stupid, and entirely lacking in the smallest sense of humanity. I would sooner have fifty unnatural vices than one unnatural virtue.'

'You are deceiving your wife!' I cried in exasperation.

'The one charm of marriage is that it makes a life of deception absolutely necessary for both parties. I deceive my wife by telling her my frequent absences are due to golf; she deceives herself by believing me. The Cloister or the Café, that is my life; I tried the Hearth, but it was a failure.'

Holmes's manner had cooled, and putting a period he remarked, 'I cannot understand how a gentleman could put himself into such a position.'

'Boredom, Mr Holmes, sheer boredom. One should always have a favourite vice: It complicates life just enough to make it interesting.'

I could not say whether this was spoken seriously. I suspect that long ago, from a desire to amuse that prompted him to throw probability out of the window for the sake of a phrase and to desert truth for the sake of an epigram, Wilde had lost the ability to distinguish between what he believed and what he said for effect—like a character in a play who feigned madness so effectively that he became mad. But the effect was extraordinary, as I recalled from the American publisher's dinner, where Wilde's words of startling wisdom had been followed willy-nilly by arrant fatuities, tumbling over each other until we gave up trying to discriminate and submitted like lotus-eaters to his dominant mind and mellifluous voice.

'I abhor the dull routine of existence,' Wilde continued. 'There are moments when the passion for sin so dominates my nature that every fibre of my body seems to be instinct with fearful impulses. But like drugs it is a taste easier acquired than gotten rid of. You know what I mean, Mr Holmes.'

'You cut life to pieces with your epigrams. Come, Watson.'

'All the Queen's horses could not hold me here longer!'

'I don't know about the Queen's horses—my tendencies don't run in that direction. But I can answer for the Queen's men, and perhaps for another man in London who lives more lives than one—at the private hotel where I have rooms to write. He is always slinking out in disguise at night, to low dens of vice and criminals' hangouts.'

'You should be prosecuted under the law which deals with those who choose your life!' I ejaculated.

'I didn't choose my life any more than my father chose his. He ruined the lives of simpleton girls by fathering bastards. Had I followed his example, Society would have looked upon me with the same indulgent eye it cast upon him. But one man's truth is another man's lie, and what appears to be our own choice is really as unalterable and inexorable as fate. I have thought of a story. Once there was a magnet and some steel filings . . .'

We had no desire to hear a story, but as soon as Wilde began, we forgot the monstrous body, the annoying habit of pulling his jowl, the yellow and irregular teeth; we were conscious only of the musical voice.

'One day the filings felt a sudden desire to visit the magnet. "Why not go today?" said one of them, but others were of opinion that it would be better to go tomorrow. Meanwhile, they began involuntarily moving closer to the magnet until, in one unanimous mass, they were swept along, and in another moment they were clinging fast to the magnet. Then the magnet smiled, for the steel filings had no doubt at all that they were paying the visit of their own free will.' Wilde broke the spell. 'And you know the Amendment Act was not directed towards me.'

'I know nothing of the kind,' answered Holmes defensively.

'It was directed towards men whose sexual appetite for little *girls* gave rise to a flourishing white-slave trade, abstracting girls from their parents and forcing them to gratify—what was Dr Watson's fine phrase?—"the unnatural lust of full-grown men". Mr Stead, editor of the *Pall Mall Gazette*, brought it to the public's attention in an article he entitled "The Maiden Tribute of Modern Babylon"—presumably to minimise the risk of increased circulation.

'The white-slave trade does not come within my horizon.'

'Nor that of Mr Labouchere, Liberal Member of Parliament, whom I always admired for his sparkling wit (which compares favourably with mine) and for his unconventional relationship with the woman posing as his wife. When the white slavery measure was debated, he amended it to punish members of the same sex who indulged in what he called "familiarities and indecencies".'

'Liberal members are not known to discourage indecency.'

'There is no such thing as a Liberal; there are only people who are Conservative about different things. The Amendment passed, with harsh and heavy penalties.

Curious how attractive humanitarian measures become, when coupled with the aggressive instinct. Men never seem to let humaneness get in the way of helping humanity.'

Wilde, pacing, noticed the nude statuette turned to the wall. He turned it back as Holmes remarked, 'It curtailed your practices.' One of the peculiarities of Holmes's proud, self-contained nature was that although he docketed fresh information quickly and accurately in his brain, he seldom made acknowledgement. I knew his present pose of indifference concealed a keen curiosity.

'You cannot change human nature by changing the law. It had no more effect than an excise tax. It didn't prevent consumption; it only made it more expensive. That is why it is called the Blackmailer's Charter. When threatened, you cannot defend yourself, for the law is as dangerous to you as the blackmailers. It is outrageous! It is intolerable! Really, if England persists in treating us like this, she doesn't deserve to have us!' Wilde was interrupted by the re-appearance of Billy, carrying a dish of pastry and looking a happier boy. 'May I have a piece of your pastry, Billy?'

The boy held out the plate, his eyes widening at sight of the statue. 'It is like the boys at Charles Second Street.'

'Yes,' said Wilde, munching on a pastry, 'there is little difference between statues. Mr Holmes and I have decided that I shall look into—'

'I have decided nothing of the kind!'

'You work for Mr Holmes as a page. Do you spend your wages wisely?'

'I give them to my mother.'

'One can never be too kind to one's mother, as I was saying to my friend, Dr Conan Doyle. His tells him to wear flannel next to his skin and never believe in eternal damnation, but mine says that there is nothing worth living for except sin. Hasn't your mother warned you against going with strangers?'

'I went to the house with Cartwright, but he wasn't a stranger.'

'You have known him for some time.' Wilde offered another pastry.

'He has brought telegrams to us, and his brother helped Mr Holmes in the case of the ghostly hound.'

'Let us not talk about him. I am not conducting an investigation. The ghostly hound. Is that a case that Dr Watson hasn't chronicled yet?'

'When Mr Holmes is away, Dr Watson invites me to his room and tells me about cases. "Ricoletti of the Club Foot and His Abominable Wife" and "The Repulsive Story of the Politician, the Lighthouse, and the Trained Cormorrant" '—Wilde fixed me with a baleful eye, as if accusing me of fabricating titles to season the interest of Holmes's real cases—'and "The Little Case of Messenger-Manager Wilson"—why, that's the manager of Cartwright's telegraph office!'

'One of my own brothers was named Wilson,' said Wilde indifferently.

'How could that be, sir?'

'My father preferred it that way. Do you go to school, Billy?'

'I am a day boy at the Board School.'

'I suppose they teach you to remember instead of teaching you how to grow. What do you study?'

'Science—'

'The record of dead religions.'

'—and history—'

'The criminal calendar of Europe, and the only form of fiction in which real characters do not seem out of place, mainly soldiers and sailors.'

'Like The Guv'nor, sir.'

'The Guv'nor,' said Wilde absently, offering the plate.

'The man who owns the house on Charles Second Street was a sailor.'

'Let us not talk about him. I suppose your school is as ugly as any other public building?'

'That's the way it's supposed to be, isn't it, sir?'

'A school should be the most beautiful place in any town—and naughty children punished by being debarred from going to school the following day.'

Billy's face brightened. 'I understand, sir. I wasn't naughty at the house, but The Guv'nor said I must never go there again.'

'And you sha'n't. But I wasn't talking about these things, was I, Mr Holmes? Billy, you must put all these thoughts out of your mind.'

'If you say so, sir,' said Billy, accepting the last pastry.

'It is clear to me, Mr Holmes, that the boy is innocent.' I was bound to agree. Any doubts about Billy's manliness had been dispelled. 'But there is some sinister purpose behind this, and I urge you to accept my assistance. I sha'n't ask for carte blanche—or carte lavande.'

'If we meet again, I should not like it to be in our lodgings.'

'A new place! May I suggest the Strangers' Room of the Diogenes Club?'

'Impossible. My brother is a member there.'

'Is he a detective, too?'

'He is with the Foreign Office.'

'I have many friends there. Where else would you suggest?'

'The Bar of Gold.'

'That opium den behind the wharves in Upper Swandam Lane, run by the rascally Lascar and his Dane companion? I wouldn't be found dead there, even in disguise. Well, you won't go anywhere nice, and I won't go anywhere vile, so where will it be, Mr Holmes—your place, or mine?' Holmes strode to the door. 'Meanwhile, if I have not heard from you, I shall proceed.'

'If we meet in public, do not acknowledge our acquaintance.'

'Our collaboration does not imply your approval of my way of life—or mine of yours.' Wilde held out his flabby hand to Billy, who, to my amaze, took it. 'Come play with Cyril and Vyvyan. What days are you clear from your duties?'

'I have a Sunday evening, sir, every month.'

'Mr Holmes is a demanding employer, isn't he? Take care of Billy, Mr Holmes. He is a lad of rare promise and hidden potential.'

'Nonsense!' I exclaimed. 'He's only—'

'We all begin as an "only", until we recognise our true nature and destiny—even Mr Holmes, who didn't realise at first that a profession might be made out of a hobby. Permit me to illustrate.' Wilde placed the statuette upon the table, its nude parts confronting us.

I protested. 'What are you doing with that disgusting—!'

'Ah, Dr Watson, what a wealth of self-denial is in that remark.'

'He's just a boy!'

'Anything is good which stimulates thought at any age.' Frantically I looked towards Holmes, but he was watching with a scientist's fascination. 'This, Billy, is Praxiteles' statue of Hermes, god of science and the arts. The original was made long ago, by a man in a different place than London.'

'With different morals!' I hastened to add.

'Many would call it "immoral". Do you think it is "immoral", Billy?'

My heart ached for the poor lad, accustomed to being told and unprepared to make a judgement. He stared intently at the statuette, then walked from side to side, viewing it from every perspective. Finally, with astonishing assurance, he pronounced, 'I think, sir—it is very well-made.'

'Bravo!' cried Wilde. 'There is no such thing as a "moral" or "immoral" work; it is either well-made or badly-made. Anything is well-made if it has some quality of wit or beauty, and a sense of beauty is the highest sense of which a human being is capable. You are wasting your life in the page-boy business, Billy. One day you will be the foremost art critic in London, and I shall have to compromise my contempt for critics and worship at your feet.'

'See here!' I cried, outraged by the worshipful wonder with which Billy was regarding Wilde. I seized the boy by his hand and marched him to the door.

Wilde seated himself and, leaning back in a posture of easy triumph, blew a smoke ring. 'The evidence is complete. It is an infallible litmus test.'

As we passed through the door, Wilde's mocking voice pursued us. 'You will excuse me if I do not rise to see you out.'

CHAPTER THREE

❧

Result of a Fruitless Inquiry

'What an amazing day to be riding through this grey, monstrous city of ours, with its myriads of people, its sordid sinners, and its splendid sins!' Wilde had not stopped talking since, in response to a noon-time telegram, Holmes and I had stepped into his cab.

After we had left Wilde's house the day before, I had not seen Holmes until evening. The haggard face which he displayed upon returning informed me that he had found the world of Wilde's tendencies inaccessible to his usual avenues of investigation. 'I have had a blank day, Watson,' he said.

'We all need help sometimes.' His withering look told me that he did not feel it was a fact of nature that applied to him. Holmes was not a man to lose easily. His personal pride as well as his sense of professional competency suffered keenly from the prospect of defeat, so I felt sure that in extremity he would accept Wilde's help. Now, shortly after noon of the day following our interviews with

Wilde, we were jostling along in a four-wheeler, while he held forth interminably.

'Strange that although town life nourishes and perfects all the more civilised elements in man, a modern city is the exact opposite of what everyone wants. The cities I saw in America were even worse.'

'I have lived in San Francisco!' I rebuked him.

'It is odd, but everyone who disappears is said to be seen in San Francisco. It must be a delightful city, with all the attractiveness of the next world. Well, Mr Holmes, I take it you spent the whole of yesterday drawing every cover and picking up no scent—my metaphor is borrowed from the hunt.'

'It is nothing to a man's discredit if he has a blank day,' I interposed.

'Every man has his limitations. It cures us of the weakness of self-satisfaction.'

'I have a clear day,' Holmes was stung into replying, 'and I am willing to look into your friend's case, so long as it is understood that I commit myself to nothing.'

'Where are we going?' I enquired.

'To the Buckingham Palace—'

'The Palace!' My mind reeled. 'We're not properly dressed.'

'If we are going to Buckingham Palace,' said Holmes, 'your friend is indeed noble.'

'You are not far out about both,' replied Wilde. 'I see that you find the case more interesting at once. But of course, you have spent your entire life preserving those laws which in England are not the defenders of the weak and the poor, but ramparts for the aristocracy, who regard exploitation as their natural right.'

'You enjoy their company,' said Holmes testily.

'I suppose Lady Queensberry told you. It is monstrous the way people go about saying things behind one's back that are absolutely true. I do like aristocrats: They have the redeeming grace of realising that manners are of more importance than morals. You do not go out into Society much?'

'I loathe every form of Society.'

'I love it. It is food and drink and oxygen to me. Why are we stopping? I suppose the Suffragettes are marching. My friend Dr Conan Doyle calls them "only men dressing up like women." Oh, I beg your pardon, Mr Holmes.' He thrust his head out the window. 'No, it is the Socialist demonstration that Mr Shaw spoke about yesterday at the Café Royal—where all sensible Socialists dine.'

'Socialism's aim is egalitarian mediocrity,' said Holmes, 'and mediocrity hates genius. I am surprised at your inconsistency.'

'We are never more true to ourselves than when we are inconsistent.'

'Ungrateful rabble,' I remarked.

'The best among the poor are always ungrateful. Also, discontented, rebellious, and disobedient. They are quite right to be, so long as Society recommends that the poor improve their lot by thrift—like advising a starving man to eat less. Will you look, Mr Holmes? You may not see any clients, but you will see future criminals. Contrary to moralists' views, most criminals are what ordinary people would be if they hadn't got enough to eat.'

'You would not think to look at them, Watson,' said Holmes, 'but I suppose they all have a little immortal spark concealed about them.'

'That is quite true,' I agreed.

'Nothing is ever quite true,' remarked Wilde. The cab lurched into motion. 'Have you read my essay, "The Soul of Man Under Socialism"? I regret that a portion of our society is practically in slavery, but I cannot agree either with Society, which tries to solve the problem by amusing the slaves, or with Socialists, who propose to solve it by enslaving the entire community—stupidity, aggravated by good intentions. If Socialism is to have any value, it must lead to Individualism. But if the end is authoritarian, man's last state will be worse than the first.'

'Authority is our bulwark against Anarchists and Dynamiters.'

'You consider our society the best of all worlds: everyone firmly and reassuringly in his place. But you violated that natural order when you helped Lady Queensberry. Surely you realise that the Scarlet Marquess hates you with such fury because you threatened the order which protects his hereditary pleasures and privileges. You rose above your station in life. Ah, Hyde Park Corner. What a marvellous statue of Achilles, for those of us who share Achilles's tendencies. Isn't it wonderful, Dr Watson, how the sculptor caught all the details?'

Instead of turning up Constitution Hill towards the Palace, we continued down Grosvenor Place.

Wilde noted my alarm. 'When Mr Holmes said we were going to Buckingham Palace, I said he was not far out. I did not say he was correct.'

'This is playing with words,' said Holmes testily.

'Which is *my* game, one at which you cannot best me.' Wilde spied a troop of soldiers marching from Knightsbridge. 'Look at those bullet heads, close-cropped and red-eared, with flushed bruiser faces. What a sense of high-blooded animalism they leave behind them!' I had often heard men speak of 'a damned fine-looking woman', but I had never heard one speak so of another man.

'Those are the Queen's soldiers!' I exclaimed.

'They are,' replied Wilde absently, 'frequently.' We rode in silence until we turned the corner at Victoria Station. 'We are close to our destination,' said Wilde. 'I must tell you now that my client will be wearing a mask. To you, this is merely another adventure, but to him, who bears a name that is a household word all over the earth, it is a matter of survival or disgrace. I ask you, on your honour, not to try to trace his identity.'

'The Buckingham Palace *Hotel*!' I exclaimed as we pulled up.

'You see, you were not far out,' said Wilde.

'You have not been direct with me,' rebuked Holmes.

'You need have no reservations. The cab will be waiting.'

'Do you always keep the cab waiting?' I enquired.

'If it is a good cab. Well, Mr Holmes?'

I could not guess from Holmes's inscrutable face whether he would continue or abandon the enterprise. But my hunter's instinct was urging me on, and I wagered it was the same with him.

After a long pause he said, 'Come, Watson. We shall give Mr Wilde's mysterious friend five minutes to convince us.'

We stepped out of the cab—into one of the most singular and dangerous adventures of Holmes's career.

CHAPTER FOUR

An Ignoble Surprise

I had heard that the Buckingham Palace Hotel was the
most luxurious in London, but the room to which Wilde
led us was as plain as the reception room of an office.
Wilde apologised. 'This is not how a gentleman should
live, but my friend is ascetic.' Wilde had no sooner spoken
than a door opened and the man himself appeared. He
was below medium height and dressed in a solemnly
respectable regulation frock-coat with a gold Albert chain
across the waistcoat. Between greying brown hair and a
full beard, his face was covered by a black mask.

'Have you brought me poison, Mr Wilde?' he asked in
a melancholy, satirical voice, with a vaguely Germanic
accent.

'I have brought you the sovereign antidote: Mr
Sherlock Holmes.'

'I should have preferred poison.'

'Come, now,' chided Wilde. 'Suicide is the greatest

compliment one can make to society, but being dead must be the most boring experience in life.'

'I am not a believer in your powers,' said the masked man to Holmes.

'Fortunately, they are not dependent upon your belief. Can you not deal direct, without a mask?'

'They are often more revealing than faces,' interposed Wilde. 'Give a man a mask and he will tell you the truth.'

'How shall I address you?' demanded Holmes of the masked man.

'Poor—unfortunate—miserable—'

'Your state of mind is immaterial. You are noble—'

'Why, Mr Holmes, whatever gave you that idea?'

'*You* said he was noble, Mr Holmes,' interposed Wilde quickly. 'I said you were not far out.'

'I have been brought here under false pretenses.' Holmes's voice was glacial.

'In the name of God!' cried the man in an ecstasy of despair. 'Save me if you can! I am faced with a fate worse than death, for it means disgrace as well. I am not a well man, Mr Holmes. There is a weak place in my heart, and it will not take much to knock me over.'

'In a minute you have progressed from threats of suicide to concern for your health. I think we may see our way clear to make further progress.' The effect of Holmes's words was miraculous. As so often before, his masterful personality dominated the situation, transforming it to his will. The masked man held out his hand. An expression of singular intentness came over Holmes's face, and his eyes fixed with eager curiosity upon the hand for a long moment before he shook it. 'Who is this?' asked the masked man.

'My friend and colleague, Dr Watson. You may say before him anything which you may say before me.' As I pressed the man's hand, I noted with alarm that it was damp and cool to the touch. The face visible below his vizard was white, while his lips were tinged with a shade of blue. Obviously he was in the grip of some chronic and deadly disease. 'Please arrange your thoughts,' said Holmes, 'and let us know exactly what has occurred.'

The masked man seated himself and began his singular narrative: 'You must know that my affairs are large beyond the belief of ordinary men. I travel widely, and my correspondence requires that I have a private secretary fluent in many languages.'

'A male secretary, of course.'

'I have little to do with the fair, though generally homely, sex. I suppose you are within your rights in asking.'

'We will agree to suppose so.'

'A secretary seldom remains with me for long, and when he leaves I reward him with a token of appreciation: a house or small business.'

'A generous reward, indeed.'

'I shall pass over insignificant details—'

'What seems of little consequence to one person may appear of greatest consequence to another. You have already told me so much that the rest may be superfluous.'

With a bewildered look, the masked man resumed: 'A month ago, finding myself without a secretary in London—'

'—The centre of your affairs—' prompted Holmes.

'I endeavoured to avoid my worries by attending the St James's Hall. After the interval I lingered in the bar.'

'Mr Holmes,' interrupted Wilde, 'you may not have observed that the clientele there is homogeneous.'

'I became aware of a young man, as good-looking as ever I saw in my life, with alert and graceful manner, a comely face, and well-dressed appearance. Our eyes met, he spoke to me, and soon we were conversing like old friends. He was from Sudbury, in Suffolk, and although he had come up to London to make his fortune, he still found himself unemployed. You may guess that I concluded he could fill the vacant post of my secretary. As the Hall was emptying, he invited me to the home of his uncle, with whom he was stopping.'

'An old Persian saying,' Holmes interposed: ' "There is danger for him who taketh the tiger cub"—'

'Excuse me,' interrupted Wilde again, 'the correct wording is, "There is danger for him who goeth *with* the tiger cub". At least it should be. One never knows what may happen in *his* den.'

'When we arrived at a private house in Charles Second Street, the young man explained that his uncle would return soon. It was warm in the drawing room, and he suggested that we remove our coats.' From the corner of the black silk vizard, a bead of perspiration appeared and trickled down his cheek. The part of his face that was visible below the vizard began turning more ashen, his thin hands trembled, and his breathing became more laboured. 'Mr Holmes, you will forgive me. I find it difficult.' He gestured helplessly. 'We were seated side-by-side upon the sofa. The young man admired my watch, an heirloom which I inherited from my father.' The masked man withdrew from his waistcoat pocket a timepiece, then suddenly checked himself and returned it. 'The young man asked to look at it more closely. As I passed it to him, it slipped from our hands into his lap and thence to the cushion. I went down to retrieve it. . . .' A Niagara of perspiration coursed down the man's cheeks, and his voice vibrated with horror. 'At that precise moment, the door flew open to admit a man of middle years and military bearing. His smile of welcome quickly turned to surprise, then shock, then horror, and finally to intense anger. The young man leapt to his feet, stammering explanations, but the man would hear none of them. He bellowed at us: accusations, threats. He ordered me to leave the house. I rushed—rushed to—to—' Suddenly, with a convulsed expression, the masked man sprang out of his chair, clawing at the furniture to hold himself erect with one hand, while with the other tugging at his collar. He relapsed backwards.

'It's his heart, Holmes!' I exclaimed, leaping to the man's side and tearing open his collar.

'My medicine,' he gasped.

'Nitroglycerine? I have my own.' I placed one of my pills under his tongue. Soon, his breathing became regular and his skin returned to a more healthy colour. I reached to remove the silk mask, but he seized my arm. Only the Angel of Darkness would reveal his identity. It was clear to me that I would be wise to augment my supply of medicine from the chemist's across the way, so seizing up my hat and cloak and calling back to Holmes, 'Keep him sitting,' I fled out the door.

And now, I will intrude my own insignificant personality to explain something that might otherwise confuse the reader. After I had left, things took place which the reader must know. The best solution was for Holmes to write his account, which I could insert here. 'If you really want to spend your retirement writing a dissertation on detecting,' I told him, 'the sooner you begin honing your writing skills the better. I have just reached the beginning of the chapter at the hotel. I will write what happened up to the point where I departed, while you write what followed.' I cleared the drop-leaf table and laid out two sheaves of foolscap and pens. 'We shall sit at opposite ends and write together.'

Holmes circled the table like a hunting dog sniffing the gorse. 'Will I need to fill *all* that foolscap?'

'Of course not. Sometimes one throws away quite a lot.'

'*I* sha'n't.'

'Of course not,' I reassured him. I must admit to malice in my method. For fourteen years I had laboured to please Holmes by chronicling his adventures and triumphs, yet all I had ever heard from him was that I had degraded what should have been a course of lectures into a series of tales, emphasizing human elements to the detriment of rational niceties. 'Cut out the poetry, Watson!' he would say. Well, Mr Know-all, I thought, now you shall find at first hand how difficult it is. 'You must get everything together before you begin, or you will devise interruptions,' I advised him.

'You needn't speak to me as if I were a child. How long should it take?'

'Half an hour at most,' I answered treacherously. 'Commence.' I had scarcely written 'Chapter Four: An Ignoble Surprise. I had heard that the Buckingham Palace Hotel was the most luxurious in London . . .' when I became aware that Holmes was shaking his pen. 'What's wrong?'

'This pen.'

'Nonsense. I gave you the best one.'

'It doesn't fit my hand well.'

'Your hand will accommodate.' I resumed: '. . . but the room to which Wilde led us was as plain as the . . .'

Holmes rose from his chair. 'Where are you going?' I demanded.

'I have no matches to light my pipe.'

'You must write a bit before you reward yourself with a fill.'

With a resentful glance he returned to his seat, and I heard the continuous scratching of pen across foolscap as I resumed: '. . . reception room of an office. Wilde apologised: "This is not how a gentleman should live, but my friend is ascetic".' I was interrupted by the sound of foolscap being wadded up. 'What is the trouble?'

'It is not my best work.'

'Good. We can't all be Shakespeare. Go it again.'

'*Again*?' he replied in appalled tone.

'Do get on with it, Holmes!' With a resentful glare he bent to his page. By this time I could see that events were following a pleasing course. Slowly, painfully he inserted one word after another onto the page. Then: 'How do you spell—?'

'Never mind the spelling!'

'I should not like to—'

'Holmes, this is procrastination!' He rose. 'Where are you going?'

'To consult one of my monographs for the name of—'

'Write *first*; research *later*! At this rate you will not be finished by the time that I reach my departure.' I resumed: 'Wilde had no sooner spoken than a door opened and the man himself appeared.' I became aware that Holmes was standing behind my shoulder. I am not one to write a clean first draft, but now I took care that not a blot or cross-out would mar the miraculous flow of words onto the page. I was almost asphyxiated by a cloud of tobacco smoke, directed towards my left ear. 'Holmes! This is unworthy of you!'

'You needn't be sharp.' He seated himself again. My writing hand was stiffening, so to relieve it I rose and unobtrusively circled the table, coming to rest behind Holmes. He stopped. 'I cannot write with someone looking over my shoulder.' I retreated to the sideboard, where I brewed myself a whisky and soda from the gasogene. Suddenly, Holmes threw down the pen with such violence that it flew off the table and rolled across the bear-skin rug. 'This is *hard work*!'

'Indeed. How could I have escaped discovering that fact in chronicling twenty-six of your cases?'

'Leave the deuced stuff out!' He leapt up and paced to the fireplace. My feelings of triumph were immediately countered by concern for the story. It could hardly be understandable without the facts which only Holmes could provide. I adopted a conciliatory tone.

'Let us stick to our lasts. Mine is writing and yours is detection.'

'Agreed!' he responded.

'But so there will be no breach in the story, perhaps you will give me an oral sketch of events, from the time I left the hotel to the moment when I rejoined you and Wilde in the street.'

Holmes's eyes were suspicious. 'I sha'n't have to write anything?'

'I shall take it down myself, word-for-word.'

'As I dictate it?' Holmes's voice was unnaturally eager.

'Just relate it as if you were speaking to a friend.'

'Agreed.' Holmes flung himself down upon the sofa and leaned back. 'Thedoorhadhardlyclosedafteryou-Watsonwhenanotherdooropenedandacomelyyoung—'

'Holmes!'

He glanced at me with infuriating innocence. 'Am I going too fast?'

I dared not reply, for the fate of the story hung in the balance. With a self-satisfied smile, Holmes resumed at slower pace:

'The door had hardly closed after you, Watson, when another door opened and a comely young man entered. He had flaxen hair and striking blue eyes, a weak, sensitive mouth, and a manner which combined shyness with a brash overlay of assertiveness. He was carrying a pair of boots that I yearned to get my hands on, for the soles bore a peculiar clay. (Alas, how I have to show my hand when I tell the story.) Seeing his master's distress, he dropped the boots and rushed to him, crying, "I shall get your medicine."

'"I have already taken it," said the masked man. "This is Sherlock Holmes."

'"But, sir, we agreed it was too dangerous—"

'I looked up from examining the boots to see Wilde staring at the boy across the chair in which sat our client, still gasping for breath. "Haven't I seen you before?" enquired Wilde. "At the Alhambra, perhaps, or the Royal Theatre of Varieties? Would you care to join me for luncheon at the Café Royal? Mr Holmes, whatever are you doing in that semi-recumbent posture?"

'By this time I had gratified my curiosity about the shoes, and I asked our client if he wouldn't prefer continuing at another time. "My heart pounds like a horse's," he replied, "but thank God for the medicine. To come to the end of my story: I rushed from the house like one possessed. It was not until I reached my hotel that I realised I had left my watch behind. The next day I made discreet inquiries. The young man had removed from the house that morning. I resigned myself to the loss of my father's watch, with its loving inscription. A day later, glancing through the journals, I caught sight of an advertisement in the Personals sheet. It was headed, 'To the Man with the Watch', and it begged my address so the watch might be returned. Here, this is it."

'I glanced at the clipping and said, "This is from the *Times*." The man was, of course, astounded. "The detection of types is one of the most elementary branches of knowledge to the special expert in crime," I explained. "You replied by advertising in the *Times*."

'"Yes, and my watch was promptly returned by the young man, with apologies for his uncle's behaviour. It was a vindication of my faith in the goodness of all men—except myself. There is no more to tell."

'As you know, Watson, I am too experienced to be deceived by such a ruse, especially when accompanied by that sulky defiance which goes with concealing guilty knowledge. "One should never be less than candid with one's detective or one's doctor," I prompted him. "You should know that, Doctor." You start, Watson. You didn't suspect the man was a brother medico? I must refresh your memory about the visible indications. But the man immediately replied, "I am not a doctor," and Wilde smirked at my *lapsus linguae*.

'The masked man resumed: "A week later my secretary—I had filled the post meanwhile with a young man who was willing to come for half-wages—called my attention to another advertisement. My blood froze. It was cunningly worded, and referred offensively to one of my former secretaries, even quoting from my letter to him. The next day, another advertisement, concerning another secretary."

' "You have the advertisements, of course?" I asked him.

' "I—burned them all. I never imagined it would come to *this*, a letter which arrived a week ago, along with one of mine to a former secretary." He handed the secretary letter to Wilde and the other to me. It was the usual demand for money or "all your letters will be made public, with details of your other activities." When I remarked that "activities" must refer to the St James's, he shook his head. "How could they know about that?"

' "The young man, or the uncle—"

' "They have said nothing. The young man has assured me."

'I could scarcely conceal my excitement as I enquired, "You have been directly in contact with him?"

'"He is as appalled as I at these infamous events."

'"What do you make of the letter to his secretary?" I asked Wilde. He read out a phrase: "'Your proficiency in French and Greek . . .'" and shrugged his shoulders. "A curious construction could be put on those terms by anyone so inclined. If letters like these fell into the hands of those who cater to an inquisitive public through the garbage papers—in the old days men had the rack; now we have the Press."

'"I swear as I hope for God's mercy!" cried the masked man, "I am innocent!"

'"We are all innocent", replied Wilde, "until we are found out."

'"You do not understand, either of you!" the man fairly shouted, his face contorted with fear. "Surely, Mr Holmes, with your world-wide reputation which you value above all else, you can understand I must be above suspicion, like Caesar's wife."

'"Caesar was known as 'the husband of every wife', said Wilde, 'and the wife of every husband'."

'"You are quick", I said, "to assert that great persons share your tendencies."

'"No quicker than you, Mr Holmes, to assume they share yours."

'I addressed the masked man. "So you are in the power of rascals who will soon inform you of ransom they intend to levy—"

'"They have already done so."

'"The price?"

'"A long one, but not beyond my means."

'"You have not paid it."

'"Another message was to provide details. It never came. Only another advertisement: 'Plans changed. Watch and wait'." It was the first surprising point of the case, Watson, indicating either a complication, or opportunity for greater profit. I enquired what further action he had taken. "The same desperate expedient that you used in a time of similar peril," he replied. "I created the impression that I had died".'

I paused in my writing and gaped at Holmes. I had related his subterfuge in escaping from the Reichenbach Fall only to my closest friends (admittedly, so often that Holmes had warned me, 'If you ever publish the account, it will be regarded as a reprint'). Apparently my friends included someone in the masked man's circle.

'Yes, Watson, a distinct touch. What Mr Wilde calls "Life imitating Art".'

'"The Press published my obituaries and leading articles about my life and character," the masked man continued. "We never know until we are dead what others think about us. I realised for the first time what a wounded name I would leave behind me. I am not a happy man. I have often thought my miserable existence should have been terminated at birth as I drew my first howling breath. I have achieved wealth beyond the dreams of avarice, but I have never known love, although I have yearned all my life for love unsullied by passions. My heart tells me my days are almost done, but I feel I have never dared to live my own life."

'"One's real life is often the life one has not led," Wilde interrupted. "Most people die of a sort of creeping common sense, and discover too late that the only things one never regrets are one's mistakes. Most people never possess their souls before they die. They are other people. Their thoughts are someone else's opinions, their lives a mimicry, their passions a quotation. But if we have any purpose here on earth, it is to realise our true selves."

'"I am not pretending to be any better than I am, but

I have never steeped my senses in degrading pleasures, nor stooped to those lower vices which are better left unsaid."

'Wilde's response to this astonished me with its force: "To regret one's desires is to put a lie into the lips of one's own life. It is no less than a denial of the soul. Of course one feels terror about passions and sensations that are stronger than oneself—sensations that have remained savage because the world has sought to starve them into submission or kill them by pain. But we are punished for our refusals. Every impulse which we strive to strangle broods in the mind and poisons us."

'Wilde's friend turned to me for comfort. "Is not my life pathetic and futile? I reach, I grasp, and what is left in my hands? A shadow—misery. Have you ever known a nightmare, Mr Holmes, in which you felt there was some all-important thing for which you searched and which you knew was there, but which remained forever just beyond your reach?"

'"I do not blame you for feeling so; I should blame you if you acted upon it."

'My remark, unfortunately, instead of terminating confessions, only stimulated more personal ones. "I should have been a poet, as I wanted to be when I was a child—a sickly child, sharing my mother's bedroom and listening to the other children outside at play. But my father said, 'Poetry is only for idle women.' I think now of the pain he must have felt at being shut out of our lives. If I had behaved differently, he might not have resented me the rest of my life when I surpassed his accomplishments. I should have liked him to be proud of me. Then, I could have been proud of myself, instead of feeling that I am inferior, like an old maid, a spinster."

* * *

'I have related this, Watson, because of your obsession with the coarse, human aspects of my cases, but naturally they will have no place in the final account.'

'Certainly, Holmes,' I replied, again noting with regret how abhorrent all emotions were to this cold, precise, admirably balanced and most perfect reasoning machine—a brain without a heart. Holmes continued:

'"Did the blackmailers believe that you had died?" I enquired.'

'Holmes,' I interrupted, 'you cannot say "enquired" again. You have already used it at least five times.'

'You are a fine one to complain about repetition, considering your interminable succession of "comelies" and "aquilines".'

'And what of your "seven different explanations"? And I shall scream if I hear again, "When you have eliminated the impossible, whatever remains"—'

'What of your Wilsons and Violets? Can *everyone* we meet be named—'

'I have 100 per-cent recall. To return to this fine point of composition: "enquired"—'

'Supply another verb. I cannot be bothered.'

'If I must do everything for you.' I went to the bookshelf. 'It would help if we had a *thesaurus*. Look at these books: *American Encyclopaedia, Continental Gazetteer,* Whitaker's *Almanack*—all yours.'

'Nothing prevents you from buying yourself a *thesaurus*.'

'Buying *myself*—!' All my frustration over Holmes's arrogance burst. 'What is wrong with *your* buying me one! You certainly profit enough from clients attracted to you by my stories in *The Strand*.'

'My chief advertisement has always been word-of-mouth from—'

'—satisfied clients? Did you consider my dear wife "satisfied", despite her inheritance being scattered from one end of the Thames to the other? Or Hilton Cubitt, shot through the heart shortly after engaging you? I cannot say what a strain it has been for me to gloss over your failures.'

'Can it really be that you believe I owe any part of my prominence as The World's Foremost Consulting Detective to *you*?'

'You have said—'

'I have said: "In noting your fallacies I am occasionally guided towards the truth." If you consider *that* an encomium . . . ! But what else could I expect from a panderer to popular taste?'

'What were you when I joined you? And what would you have been had I not?'

'What were you when I took you in? A half-pay-pension ex-Army surgeon, living off the public dole, eking out a precarious existence in a second-class—' Holmes paused dramatically '—*third*-class hotel, drinking at the Cri and squandering your pension at race-meetings—'

'When you *took me in*!'

'Stamford took pity on you when you told him you'd prefer having a partner to being alone. I could have chosen from many who—'

'—would have done nothing to advance your career, as have I! "A trusty comrade is always of use, and a chronicler more so", remember?'

'"Go halves on the diggings." *C'est à rire!* Are you aware of the expense of our comfortable bachelor lifestyle, when you come to me for your cheque-book to indulge your addiction to gambling on the turf?'

'*My* addiction! What of *yours?*'

'It is my only vice. You said so yourself in "The Yellow Face".'

'That was for public consumption. I do not air domestic matters in public.'

'Then, perhaps we should air them in private. For fifteen years this has been our home—'

'Home! This is no more your home than is the waiting-room at Paddington Station, which you briefly pass through on your way to more stimulating places. And what do you *really* do in those "five small refuges" which you admit you keep in London? And where were you *really* during the Great Hiatus?'

'Florence, Montpellier—where else should I be but pursuing—'

'Pursuing *what*, Holmes? There's a great deal more to be said.'

'Then let us say it. Have you ever wondered about that night at the St Clairs', while we were unravelling the adventure of—'

'"The Man with the Twisted Lip." I remember. I *wrote* the story.'

'Then perhaps you recall how we spent the night.'

'Mrs St Clair provided for us a room with a double bed—'

'Which you occupied—'

'—while you—' My mind refused to continue.

'Go on,' prompted Holmes with demoniacal glee. 'I collected pillows and cushions and made a sort of Eastern divan upon which I *sat up all night.*'

'Holmes!' I ejaculated. 'This is monstrous!' I fled into Holmes's bedroom and slammed the door. From outside came his taunting voice:

'Remember, I didn't start this conversation. *You* did.'

'Holmes, I shall move my things tonight.'

'Where will you go? What will you do?'

'I shall buy another practice. I shall marry again.'

'Another *kissless* marriage?'

Holmes's words pierced the door and entered my ears like daggers. I opened the door. He was standing at the mantel, filling his pipe. 'Holmes,' I said, all my fury burnt down to bitter ashes, 'I got hurt, in the war.'

'In the *shoulder*. Shall I show you in *Beeton's*?'

'I was also wounded elsewhere. I can prove it in *Lippincott's*.'

'I am uninterested in your injuries, wherever. I think it best you leave.'

'It's settled.' Fighting back tears, I looked about the room where I had spent so many happy years. 'I shall take the gasogene, of course.'

'You will *not* take the gasogene. It was a birthday gift to *me*.'

'It was *bought* on your birthday, but it was a gift to *both* of us.'

'You cannot take it. I have become accustomed to it.'

'*I* have become accustomed to it, too. You have no feelings, Holmes, or you could understand how hard it is to cast off something you had become accustomed to.'

'That is not my concern,' said Holmes, with a slight softening.

Mrs Hudson appeared at the door. 'I thought I heard loud voices.'

'Dr Watson and I were having a discussion.'

'I can't remember ever hearing the two of you speak so sharply.'

'We never have in—' a choke caught in my throat '—fifteen years.'

'Mrs Hudson, Dr Watson is leaving Baker Street.'

'On a trip, sir? But I've never known you to go off without Mr Holmes.' Confound her! Every word pierced me to the heart.

'Will you explain, Watson?'

'I . . . am leaving Baker Street for good.'

'I can't think your leaving could be good. Have you gentlemen had a misunderstanding?'

'No, Mrs Hudson,' said Holmes, 'at last it is an understanding.'

'It's a shame, after fifteen years that you've been together, including the time when you were dead, sir, and Dr Watson kept coming here. How he suffered. He can't hide his feelings; you can always see them in his face.'

'Mrs Hudson,' I interposed, 'you don't have to—'

'And Dr Watson, don't you remember that day last April when you bounded up my steps, face beaming, and cried, "He's alive! Holmes is alive!" And I said: "Yes, I know it, sir. He's been going in and out today as an old book peddler".'

'Enough!' I cried, turning so Holmes could not see my face.

'Fifteen years. Why, that's longer than many couples are together, including Mr Hudson and me. Mr Holmes says he'll work another ten years. Think of all the adventures you could still have. Think of the stories for *The Strand*. Why, I don't believe your public would allow you to separate. They love you both so much they stand outside *The Strand* offices on publication day. Come, now, I've seen more years than both of you, and I'll ask it for all of us: Won't you make up?'

Of all the moments when I felt my life hang in the balance, I had never felt such apprehensiveness. I closed my eyes and waited. 'Perhaps,' said Holmes, 'I spoke too sharply. Some things are better left unsaid.'

My heart leapt. 'Do you admit it, Holmes? Then I—'

'Stow the sentiment, Watson,' said Holmes with a grimace of distaste. 'We may agree that the matter is closed.' Mrs Hudson beamed, as well she might, for peace in the house was her prize. 'However,' added Holmes ominously, 'I am aware that everything said in this flat is reported in *The Strand*. I shall not be made to appear the unsympathetic party.'

'What is it you want, Holmes?' I begged.

"Every word written down and shown to me, before I continue my narrative.'

'I shall do it immediately.' I seized foolscap. 'Of course, by the time they finish reading it they will have forgotten what was happening with the client—'

'Mrs Hudson!'

'I'm doing it!' I wrote it, he approved it, and then he continued.

'"You gave out that you had died," I said to the masked man. "Did the blackmailers believe you?"

'He answered with a sardonic laugh. "Look in yesterday's advertisement sheet: 'We are not deceived. Expect you to fulfill bargain. Wait for instructions.' How did they learn I was alive? No one but my closest associates—"

'"They include a Judas."

'"I believe if I trust people without reservation they will be worthy of my trust."

'"When it comes to human nature," said Wilde, "always expect the worst. You will seldom, if ever, be disappointed."

'"This change of plans carries the most sinister connotations," I warned. "But you can only wait for them to come to you. Meanwhile, warn your secretaries."

'"I did, when the advertisements first appeared. The

letters went out?" he enquired of the comely secretary, who was hovering near.

'"Yes, sir, I posted them myself. It is part of my duties," he explained to me, "along with opening and sub-dividing correspondence."

'"Good fellow. Keep a sharp eye out for advertise-ments. And have these shoes cleaned. This soil—"

'"You cannot know it," said the masked man. "It is rare."

'"It is diatomaceous."

'"But how—?!" exclaimed the man, with his eyes open.

'"I can tell at a glance different soils. This is found near Hanover."

('Your eyes open, too, Watson. Our Queen is of the House of Hanover.' Holmes chuckled in hearty, noiseless fashion. 'But perhaps it is insignificant.')

'"You are a wizard!" cried the masked man. "I have just returned from inspec—that is, visiting—"

'"*Wir sind gewohnt dass die Menschen verhöhnen was sie nicht verstehen,*" I said to the young man, who gazed at me uncomprehendingly.

'"German is the most expressive language, isn't it?" said Wilde. "Except when set to music. Wagner's is the best; it is not as bad as it sounds."

'"But dare I hope?" interrupted the masked man. There was no trace of the imperious man who had spoken so rudely when we entered.

'"Some points in this case are not devoid of interest. However, I cannot see my way clear at present to give it my attention."

'"You are offended by the moral implications," he said.

'"I hope not," said Wilde. "We are not sent into this world to air our moral prejudices."

' "Your arrival gave me fresh life and hope," said the masked man, slumping. "I now resign myself to whatever Fate may send—even my death."

' "Do not look so depressed," I said, "even though *I am doing nothing*." (I raised my voice on those words. I don't suppose you can guess why, Watson.) "Meanwhile, take no step without my consent, on your honour as an English gentleman."

' "I am not English," he replied. Wilde smirked again at my second lapse, but I passed it off by saying, "Then I shall not ask you to promise. Thank you for relieving what might otherwise have been a dull day."

' "I am happy to have amused you. I suggest we close this interview." The masked man rose and, without bowing, disappeared through an inner door.

'And now, Watson, you know everything which transpired during your absence, and you may resume your narrative from the point where Wilde and I emerged from the front door of the hotel. Meanwhile, I shall brew myself a drink from my gasogene and enjoy watching you pursue your literary endeavours. At which—' Holmes smiled condescendingly '—you are not entirely inadequate.'

CHAPTER FIVE

Strange Virtue and Ominous Advice

When I returned to the hotel, Holmes and Wilde were emerging. Wilde was wroth: 'Where is my cab! I shall have to find another!' As the cab rank was a block away, it did not seem an outrageous inconvenience.

'What do you make of it, Watson?' asked Holmes.

'It seems to me most trivial—'

'In pursuing the trivial, we have blundered upon the sensational.'

'Yet you refuse the case,' said Wilde.

'I accepted it as soon as I met your friend. A considerable crime is in contemplation. He is not the end, but the means to it, and these blackguards must not be allowed to acquire an ascendancy over him.'

'What can I do to help?' enquired Wilde.

'You may inform your friend that I am pursuing the case, but in absolute secrecy, or we are lost. So far, the blackmailers have asked only a long price. Their next will be a very long price, indeed.'

'You suspect what they will ask?'

'I *know* what they will ask, and your friend will be faced with a terrible choice, one which could affect the lives of all of us.'

'You believe his story about the St James's?' I ventured.

'I believe that *he* believes it, and that is enough for me. I shall not probe into another man's mind like a pick-lock psychologist.'

'Psychology is in its infancy as a science,' said Wilde. 'I hope, in the interests of Art, it will always remain so.'

'Your friend will have much to answer for some day before the Heavenly Assizes, but not the offence of which he stands accused now.'

'Where shall we go next?' demanded Wilde.

'*We* shall go nowhere. Return to your "family residence" and bestow your infrequent company upon your wife. And if we meet in public, do not acknowledge our acquaintance.'

'I suppose you will begin by ravelling out the curious behaviour of my friend at the St James's Bar.'

'Your friend did nothing at the St James's Bar.'

'That was the curious behaviour. But of course *you* are the expert on "the criminal world of London".'

At that instant, a neat little two-horse landau with both tops up passed in front of us, and a woman's voice rang out: 'Be careful! You are in deadly danger!' The driver instantly whipped up, and the landau rolled swiftly away. Holmes was galvanised into action.

'Quick, Watson! Don't let her get away!' Without a thought for his safety, he dashed off in wild pursuit, running out among the cabs and 'buses. I am reckoned fleet of foot, but Holmes, who was always in superb physical condition despite his sedentary habits, soon left me far behind. The landau, however, had an unbeatable advantage, and soon disappeared. Holmes was livid. 'Was there ever such bad luck!' We retraced our steps, Holmes's gait more brisk than mine, for I was conscious of an alarming weight in my chest. Preoccupied as he was, he did not see me administer to myself some of the miraculous medicine. 'Did you see who it was?' Holmes demanded of Wilde, who stood upon the same spot, unconcernedly puffing upon his cigarette.

'I didn't even see the landau until it was past. But was this warning for you—or for me?'

'It could have been either—or both.'

'I have the feeling I've heard that voice,' said Wilde.

'I have the impression I've heard it, too,' said Holmes.

For a moment the two stood silent, engrossed in thought. 'It is too tedious, standing here,' said Wilde finally, and whistling up a cab from the rank he drove away.

'Good riddance!' I exclaimed. 'Where are we going now, Holmes?'

Holmes silently watched the cab until it disappeared. Then, he fairly exploded with excitement. 'To Cadogan Place! We have a few threads in our hands now, and I hope we shall find there the end of our tangled skein. Faces to the west and quick march!'

CHAPTER SIX

A *Family Circle:*
Misery, Violence, Fear

*H*alf an hour later we were ushered into the great, yellow-curtained drawing room of a fashionable residence on Cadogan Place. 'There is another caller in the study,' the butler apologised.

Holmes had ridden in silence, and I had avoided speaking to him, knowing how he loved to dominate and surprise. But now I burst out, 'I take it you know who this woman is.'

'Memory for a voice usually serves me well, when I have listened long and intently to a client. I cannot imagine how she knew where we would be, or why she chose such a method to warn us. Some terrible circumstance must have—'

'But who *is* she, Holmes?'

'She is—'

'Lady Queensberry,' announced the butler, as double doors slid back to reveal the most regal presence ever to have graced our rooms. Although she could not have been less than fifty years of age, she was still handsome. The delicate charm and beautiful colouring of her gentle, sad, flower-like face still conveyed the impression of youthful beauty, while the nobility of her bearing and gallantry of her defiant chin proclaimed her unmistakably as of that class which is the ornament and glory of the British nation.

'My dear Mr Holmes, how good of you to honour me.'

Holmes bowed in a courtly and deferential manner. Despite his dislike and distrust of the female sex, he had a remarkable gentleness and courtesy in his dealings with them. 'Lady Queensberry, it is we who are honoured.'

'I have thought of inviting you to my receptions, but I remembered your saying that you seldom go out in Society.'

'I discourage those unwelcome invitations which call upon a man either to be bored or to lie. May I enquire where your Ladyship has spent the afternoon?'

'Spent the afternoon?' repeated Lady Queensberry in a tone of alarm which she, with extraordinary effort of aristocratic self-command, strove to conceal. 'Where else but here in my home? I can hardly afford to leave it, by the terms of that Scotch law which is so hard on a woman who divorces her husband.'

'Her Ladyship has not been riding in a landau, resting her arm on the door while leaning out to speak to someone—' Lady Queensberry's hands grasped the arms of her chair, and the pink nails turned white '—thus acquiring a dash of London mud where the sleeve would extend from the coach?'

'Had you lived a few centuries ago, you would have been burned as a witch.'

'Warlock is the male equivalent. The world is full of obvious things which only I observe. With ladies, I always observe first the sleeve.'

'There is no use trying to deceive you, Mr Holmes.'

'Of course, if it is a personal matter, concerning only your Ladyship—'

'Quite the contrary. It is a matter concerning *you*.'

Holmes could hardly have been less astonished than I, but his manner was unconcerned. 'All the more reason why I should be made aware of it, so I may lift the burden from your Ladyship.'

Hope and discretion fought in the beautiful face. Then: 'It is a terrible thing to see a dreadful event preparing itself before your eyes, clearly to understand whither it will lead, and yet to be unable to avert it. I have lived in a valley of fear, knowing that any day something dreadful may occur.'

'To whom?'

'To you.' Holmes's steely grey eyes were inscrutable. 'Ever since Lord Queensberry learned of your kind assistance to me, he has been a madman. The last time I spoke with him, he told me, "Sherlock Holmes has done himself no good, for I have broken better men than he." And in one of his letters—you cannot conceive of such letters!—he has written, "Let me see this man in the mud, with my feet on his cursed face".'

'My dear Lady Queensberry, I am on guard at all times.'

Lady Queensberry shook her head sadly. 'I am certain that he has put in motion some monstrous plot, and would torment me with the anticipation as well as the accomplishment. This arrived yesterday,' she held up a bilious-green book, 'and this venomous note today.' Holmes glanced at the note, then disdainfully tossed it to me. I bent my brows over the scrawled message: 'For Sherlock Holmes: Death! Or worse!'

'Whatever could be worse than death?' I remarked in puzzlement.

'If anyone could conceive it, Lord Queensberry could.

Another thing which he said comes back to my memory: "I will not only get level with Sherlock Holmes, I will get *more* than level." Can you explain it?'

'I should be grateful not to be pressed,' said Holmes unconcernedly. I knew he was thinking of Wilde's words: 'You rose above your station in life.'

'My husband is a hunter. I have seen him pursue his quarry with relentless energy, until he ran it to ground for his fox-hounds to tear to pieces. I see him as the hunter, and you—'

'The fox, your Ladyship, a cunning animal in its own right, and often known to outwit the hunter.'

For the briefest moment, relief glanced in Lady Queensberry's face, only to be succeeded by pain. 'When I resolved to undergo the unimaginable ordeal of divorce, I hoped that I could bury the past and regain my own life. But Lord Queensberry haunts me still. He flaunts his atheism and free love as if daring Society to call him to task. Now, if there is police court business over this, I do not know how I shall survive.'

'Your Ladyship has gone through all that flesh and blood will stand. But why would he send you Langdale Pike's *Victorian Scandals*?'

'For the chapter on his family. "Old Q" with his mistresses and gambling; Lord Queensberry's father, with his gambling losses and death by his own hand; Lord Queensberry's brother, dead by his own hand in that horrible manner; my son, Francis, dead by gunshot amid horrible rumours of self-destruction. All the sordid details of our marriage: Lord Queensberry's desertion of me to pursue his obsessions with boxing and hunting and riding; his demand that I accept a *ménage à trois* with the woman whom he brought into our house in Ascot Week; even his marriage to a seventeen-year-old child and his desertion of her the day after the wedding.' The noble lady looked imploringly at Holmes. 'How can my children and I bear reading that our family is "one with which marriage is horrible and friendship fatal and that either kills itself or those it loves".'

'And Lord Queensberry—?'

'He glories in it! Because it gives me pain. That is why he sent it to me, and to his sons, who call him "that brute" and have taken my part in the separation. He has written such letters to Percy's wife that Percy has fought with him in the streets. And to my darling Bosie, whom I have always loved and protected more than my other children. Can you imagine the feelings of a young man who reads from his father: "It makes me sick to hear you called my son. But then, I never believed you really were my son"?'

Holmes ventured, 'But surely it is a brighter house without him.'

'It was a brighter house *with* him, when he first brought me home to Kinmount.' She lifted her head, and I had a vision of the vivacious and proud young woman she once was. 'He was a young lord, heir to an immense estate, handsome, a prince of the turf and the boxing ring. But he shared none of my interests: art and music and travel. He was seldom home, and I preoccupied myself with tending the children whom he rarely saw. I think my darling Bosie would be a better man if he had not felt unwanted and deserted by the father whom he worshipped. But then, my husband might have been a better man if his father had not killed himself when Lord Queensberry was no more than a boy. How much of the world's torment is caused by unhappy families, and how terrible it is when they cause madness. A dark fate runs in his family, a circle of misery and violence and fear.' The voice of the noble, tormented woman faded to a thoughtful silence, in which I pondered the anomaly that woman, presumably the more sensitive organism, could yet exhibit such strength of mind and character.

'Your Ladyship must not trouble her mind,' said Holmes. 'Lord Queensberry is one of those men who have overshot their true generation. He should have been a buck in the days of the Regency—'

'He has sold Kinmount now,' continued Lady Queensberry sadly. 'He is living a comfortless, meaningless existence in London hotels and race-courses.'

'Lord Queensberry's behaviour represents hereditary tendencies of the most diabolical kind. We are all born with a certain nature, and one's nature will out. Forgive me for sounding like Oscar Wilde.'

The effect of Wilde's name was extraordinary. 'Do not mention his name to me!' she commanded in a voice from which even Holmes flinched.

'Forgive me. I understood he was your Ladyship's friend.'

'He has no friends, only sycophants. Everyone fears and humours him; he has a tongue like an adder. A pitifully divided man, unable to reconcile his enjoyment of the privileges and pleasures of the aristocracy with his maudlin sympathies for the lower classes. "The Soul of Man Under Socialism" indeed! Have *we* no souls, we who wine and dine him and feed his atrociously inflated ego? He is like those politicians who vote with the Liberals and dine with the Tories. As for his peculiar views of morality, Bosie says, "He feeds my soul with honey of sweet bitter thought." Bosie compares their "friendship" with Plato and Socrates, David and Jonathan, Shakespeare and Willie Hewes. Bosie'—my ears caught the unmistakable tones of a mother's anguish—'says he had already formed these ideas before he met Wilde. How *could* he!'

With utmost tact, Holmes remarked, 'I see why your Ladyship would not receive him socially.'

'You have no children, Mr Holmes, to imagine that would do anything but confirm their resolve to stand together. I receive him so I may beg of him to moderate their "friendship" at least in public, before my son's character is irreparably damaged. Besides, there is Oscar's wife. I am closer to her than Oscar's mother, and I pity her, for she cannot have any idea of their relationship. She loves her husband blindly and fatally, and I grieve to think of the trials ahead of her. But for Oscar Wilde, that brute who has murdered my son's soul'—Lady Queensberry's voice rose to a fearful crescendo—'I should like to murder *him.*'

The double doors opened, revealing a grotesque figure and smiling face. 'Journeys end in lovers' meetings,' said Wilde, lumbering into the room. 'You look surprised. I am a frequent visitor here. I particularly like this room; the wallpaper sets off my hair. Most women in London furnish their rooms with orchids, foreigners, and French novels. But here we have the room of a sweet saint: fresh flowers, pictures one can look at without blushing, books that don't shock—except this one.' He indicated a large volume. '"After King Elizabeth we have Queen James." When I think of all the harm this book has done, I despair of ever writing anything to equal it.'

'Oscar,' said Lady Queensberry, 'if my prayers are answered—'

'Prayer should never be answered. If it is, it ceases to be prayer and becomes a correspondence.' Wilde flourished a sheaf of letters. 'I have been reading the Mad Marquess' latest letters to Bosie: "Miserable" should not have a zed and "reptile" should not have two l's. His admission that he "committed a crime by bringing such a creature into the world" may be used as evidence, if he is ever brought to bar. He writes as he speaks: in crimson hieroglyphics.' Wilde shuffled through the papers. 'As for

his letters to you, he obviously takes great joy in their
composition, and in nearly every joy cruelty has its place.
With Lord Queensberry, vulgarity begins at home: He
leads you to the latrine and locks you in. Would you care to
read them, Mr Holmes?'

'I don't know whether they concern the censor or the
public prosecutor.'

'Both would find them within their jurisdiction. You
have never met the Screaming, Scarlet Marquess?'

'Only in the trail of his infamies, which I followed.' (In
this regard, I had the advantage of Holmes. At the
Criterion Bar, where followers of the turf gathered, I was
once accosted by a man with crude dress and uncouth
manners. Upon learning that I had written the adventure
of 'Silver Blaze' he insisted upon discussing the horse's
famous ancestor, whom he called 'Isomdomy'. When I
later enquired who he was, I was told, 'That's the most
dare-devil rider in England, the Marquess of Queensberry.'

Wilde enlightened Holmes: 'He resembles a stableman more than a noble lord, with twisted lip and half-
witted grin, like a character in a West-Country legend. In
his youth he pursued all the decent vices with a zeal that
placed him between Gilles de Retz and the Marquis de
Sade, but in advancing age he exhibits the decay of a really
remarkable depravity. And those are the views of his
friends.'

'I cannot allow you to speak of Lord Queensberry that
way,' reproved the gentle lady. 'I never criticise him to my
sons; he is their father. You are one, and can understand
that no father wants to see his son turn out badly.'

'We all do that. Must we discuss domestic matters
before strangers?'

'Mr Holmes has my entire trust. I do not know how he
happens to know you. Bosie told me only that you were

going at noon to the Buckingham Palace Hotel. But I
know of danger to Mr Holmes, and I have warned him.
Thanks to Bosie's cousin, I also know that Lord Queensberry is planning some mischief for the first night of your
play. You see, Mr Holmes, we are a house divided against
itself, with spies in each other's camps.'

'Spies are of no use today,' said Wilde. 'Their work is
done by the Press.'

'You must not joke about this. You know of Bosie's
insulting letters to his father.'

'His firm replies to his father's own insulting letters.'

'Do you call writing his father "What a funny little
man you are" anything but baiting a dangerous man?
They both have in their blood the love of a scene and a
tragedy. They are both filled with self-love, self-pity,
arrogance, and violent temper, and in both of them love
and hatred are so mixed that I do not believe they know
the difference. Do you not realise that Bosie is defending
you at the risk of your life? You know the talk which your
"friendship" has encouraged.'

'From the Marquess' entourage of horsy hangers-on,
bruisers of the fancy, common gamblers, and camp followers, who poison his mind.'

'Bosie must some day take his place in Society, instead
of living a life of idleness and self-indulgence.'

'Since going with me he has given up gambling and
race-meetings—'

'To replace them with interminable luncheons at the
Café Royal, where you encourage his vanity and extrav-
agance.'

'I cannot allow you to speak that way about Bosie.'

'You cannot allow me!'

'I tell him, "Nobody has the right to be unkind to his
mother".'

'Thank you for defending me to my son!'

'I may have to defend Lord Queensberry *from* his son, now that Bosie is carrying a gun and will not hesitate to use it. It went off in the Berkeley, and I tried to warn him that any weapon he might use against his father could be just as dangerous to himself or to other innocent people. I am caught between them—'

'In a trap of your own devising. I am not demanding you break off your "friendship". Only, as I warned Lord Queensberry, to be more discreet.'

'I will not be compared to him, nor will I hear more against Bosie.'

Lady Queensberry touched the bell. 'Very well. I have warned you, as I have warned Mr Holmes. You both stand in fearful danger. You must each use your own judgement—or lack of it.'

'We need not trespass upon your Ladyship's patience longer,' said Holmes.

'It has been pleasant seeing you again.' The double doors opened, and Lady Queensberry moved towards them. 'Oscar, tell Constance that I shall expect her at my reception. And you, too, if you are not playing golf.' As Lady Queensberry turned in the door to face us, I thought I had never seen such a queenly presence. 'Mr Holmes, I hope you will feel free to protect yourself. But whatever harm Lord Queensberry has done to me, I wish him no harm. Any pain caused him will be my pain, and any misfortune that falls upon his head will redound upon mine and those of my children. I rely upon your discretion.'

Looking Wilde full in the face, she added, 'And Oscar, please consider this: However painful it is to bear with the Marquess of Queensberry, think how much more painful it is to *be* the Marquess of Queensberry.'

Through a moist veil which descended over my eyes, I watched the queenly figure disappear through the doorway, and the double doors silently close behind her.

CHAPTER SEVEN

A Private Invitation

'I t is difficult to touch purity without being defiled,' remarked Wilde when we regained the street. 'Lady Queensberry is too gentle and good for the *rôle* which life has assigned to her. The world is a stage, but the play is badly cast.'

'Kindly remember that,' said Holmes forcefully, 'when tempted to denigrate the aristocracy. They are our bulwark against English decadence; they remind us of our duty.'

'Has anyone told you, Mr Holmes, that you are "*plus royaliste que le roi*"?'

'Has anyone told you, Mr Wilde—!' Holmes flashed with such anger that I feared an ugly confrontation.

'What o'clock is it?' I asked quickly. Holmes spun about and strode away, towards Sloane Square.

'I have no watch,' replied Wilde, 'and the sun is always hours in advance. I rely on the unreliable moon.'

I hurried after Holmes, who had come to a stop in the

Square, his anger spent. 'A word with you, Watson.' He linked his arm in mine and walked me back and forth, talking with barely-suppressed emotion. 'Of all our cases, we have had none more fantastic than this. We are getting some cards in our hands, and I begin to have a dim perception of the truth. This Queensberry matter, like that of Wilde's friend, may turn out to be more subtle than I suspected.'

''Ullo, luvs!' As Holmes and I had been walking, a flamboyantly-dressed man had entered the Square and stood observing us. Now, he advanced upon us. ''Ullo, luvs. A fine-lookin' couple. I c'n see y're my men an' I'm y'rs, if you catch my meanin'.' He handed us calling cards. 'I repr'sent The Private 'Ouse in Charles Second Street: genteel surroundin's an' comf'table cribs f'r spoonin', stunners f'r ev'ry taste, all prinked up or all peeled off. Live ent'rtainm't nightly, t' get the sap risin', if you catch my meanin'.' The card bore an address, and the notation *Poses Plastique*. I enquired what it meant, instantly regretting my question as the man performed a series of poses, like a strong man displaying his physique, with his hand cupped over his private parts. He opened his fingers and winked.

I flung down the card. 'I cannot believe this is happening in London!'

'Very good, sir. You're not obvious, but you've got th' Aura.' He addressed Holmes. 'When you get th' urge, f'rget 'Yde Park an' skatin' rinks an' 'specially the St James's Bar. Bring y'r privates t' the Private 'Ouse. Y'r urge an' a piece o' tin—we're the place to' spend 'em both, if you catch my meanin'. Pleased t'v made y'r acquaintance. An' if you don't min' a bit o' well-meant advice, be more discreet about that arm-in-arm in the street. It makes th' other kine nervous.' He sauntered away, almost colliding with Wilde, who had followed us to the Square.

'Holmes, this city of London is nothing but a cesspool of corruption!'

'You are in luck,' said Wilde, strolling to join us. 'But I advise you against using your tickets; you haven't the aptitude.'

'I think we can pursue this investigation better without your remarks,' said Holmes. 'We hunt in couples, not threes. And if we should meet in public—'

'I shall not acknowledge acquaintance. Will you join me for luncheon at the Café Royal? You would find it advantageous. No? Then I'll leave you to "hunt in couples". I hope you find your man.'

'Some people's affability,' said Holmes as Wilde's cab disappeared, 'is more deadly than the violence of coarser souls.'

'Where are we off to now? Charles Second Street?'

'I fancy my researches will eventually lie in that direction, but for now I have a few insignificant errands and you are not coming.'

'Then you are not going.'

'There is no prospect of danger, or I should not stir without you. In the hour of action I shall turn to you for aid. Sarasate is playing at the St James's Hall to-night. Shall we trust each other until then?'

Deceived by Holmes's casual tone and cowed by his masterful manner, I acquiesced. 'But I shall not be satisfied,' I called after him, 'until I see you back in Baker Street—' adding, with a sudden sense of foreboding '—safe—and sound.'

CHAPTER EIGHT

Doings in the Street

*L*ondoners were astonished, later that afternoon, to
see a middle-sized, strongly-built gentleman running
down Baker Street, throwing up his hands to passing cabs,
and cursing aloud as the jarveys whipped up to put
distance between them and a seeming lunatic. But I must
not get ahead of the story. As Holmes says, 'Things must
be done decently and in order.'

After Holmes left me at Sloane Square, I spent several
hours in the front window of my Pall Mall club, reading
journals and gazing at the ever-changing kaleidoscope of
great, hand-made London. But my mind was distraught
with worry for Holmes, so presently I betook myself to the
Turkish bath.

Stamford, my young dresser at Barts when I was
house-surgeon, had introduced me to the baths, and later
when I was invalided back from Afghanistan, shattered in
mind and body and feeling lonely in the great city, I often
went there to enjoy the company of men as friendless as

myself. Later, I had introduced Holmes to the bath, during one of those periods when the press of difficult cases was straining his constitution so much that I feared a breakdown. At first, he had refused, as he always did at any suggestion that his powers were limited and should be husbanded. But I convinced him by explaining that the Turkish bath is what we medical men call an alternative—a fresh starting-point, a cleanser of the system. This idea appealed to his orderly mind. Once having tried it, he found it pleasing, and afterwards the two of us went so often to Nevill's that Holmes jocularly referred to us as Companions of the Bath.

To my delight, I found it was not only therapeutic to his system but felicitous to our friendship. Over a smoke in the pleasant lassitude of the drying-room, lying side-by-side on two couches, partly covered by a sheet, he became less reticent and more human than anywhere else. There is no place to know a man better than at the bath.

Today, however, without Holmes beside me, I felt none of its soothing benefits, so I left and walked down Northumberland Avenue towards the cab rank next to the newspaper kiosk in Trafalgar Square. I had nearly reached it when I heard from a passing cab the unmistakable voice of Oscar Wilde saying, 'Stop at that kiosk.' Although he had not seen me, in a moment he would descend and subject me to another interminable discourse. Looking about for escape, I noted that buildings near the kiosk, apparently being renovated, were fenced off from the pavement by a hoarding of rough planks, some of which hung loose. Acting upon impulse, I stepped through one makeshift door.

'Have you late journals?' Wilde enquired of the kiosk.

'Any minute, sir,' replied a boyish voice. By this time I realised the foolishness of my position, but my hopes that Wilde would quickly leave were dashed.

'Haven't I seen you with Alfred Taylor?' asked the boyish voice.

'I take tea in his rooms in Little Cottage Street.'

'That's a very rough neighbourhood, isn't it, sir?'

'Perhaps. It is very near the houses of Parliament.'

'Is it true he has double curtains over the windows so the light never comes in, and he burns perfume all the time?'

'Where have you heard this?'

'From Charlie Parker, a gentleman's servant. Taylor told Charlie he could get money in a certain way if he wanted to.'

'We dined at Kettner's. Charlie loves iced bottles of "boy".'

'"Boy", sir?'

'Haven't you heard champagne called "boy"?'

'I can't imagine why.'

'Perhaps because they behave the same way when you pop their cork.'

'Very good, sir. Fred Atkins told me he came to Paris with you to meet a nephew of the Solicitor-General's wife.'

'I suppose it's true, if he told you.'

'Walter Grainger said you gave him a silver cigarette case.'

'Boys of his class smoke a lot. How else would he carry his cigarettes? You seem puzzled.'

'We're not in the same class of Society as you.'

'I don't care what any person is in Society, when he is in my society.'

'That's not the usual principles of your class, sir.'

'I like persons better than principles, and I like persons without principles better than anything. Why are you asking?'

'I'm hard up myself. I don't have money, but I spend a

lot, if you catch my meaning. If a gentleman took a fancy
to me, I'd be agreeable.' I could not believe my ears. I
knew that boys in London were enlisted into immoral acts,
but I never imagined that any solicited them. Trapped, I
had no choice but to listen, and I found that by putting my
eye to a knothole I could see everything but the interior of
the kiosk.

'I like young men who are modest and nice in appearance, and you have pleasing manners. But I do not enlist.'

'I'm known to be "so".'

'You're not the kind that ends up baying for boots?'

'Atkins says you don't care what you pay if you fancy a
chap.'

''Ullo, luvs!' The new voice, beyond the kiosk, was
female. Shifting my eye, I could see her: a woman of the
streets, in tawdry finery, with a ratty boa about her neck.
She was accosting two men coming from the bath: 'Like
some comp'ny, luvs? Special rate f'r threesomes.' The men
linked arms and passed her by. 'Why don't you try
somethin' diff'rent?' she bawled after them, in a thick voice
betraying the effects of drink. Then she wove her way
through the traffic towards us. Her face was youthful, but
so worn with sin and sorrow that one could read the
terrible years which had left their mark upon her. ''Ullo,
luv,' she greeted Wilde. Then, 'Oh, cripes, another one!
They're breedin' like ersters. 'Ow d'you *do* it?'

'I beg your pardon,' said Wilde politely.

'If th' 'ole world turns pansy, 'oo'll drop the babies f'r
you t'enlist?'

'My dear woman—'

'I'm nobody's "dear". Why don't you try somethin'
new, duckie?'

'I have tried it,' said Wilde pleasantly. 'It was like cold
mutton.'

'Aaaaaaooooow! That's a fine thing t'say t' a lydy.'

'I wouldn't to a lady,' said Wilde in his most charming manner, 'but I would to a woman who is abusing me.'

'I c'd teach you books about abuse, duckie, beginnin' wi' th' one m'own father read me b'fore I knew th' alphabet. But there's laws t' p'tect decent folks like us against y'r kine.'

'Evening, Constable,' came the kiosk boy's warning voice.

'Is this woman bothering you, sir?'

'I can't say I noticed her.'

'It's this Liberal permissiveness. Even the Prime Minister went about truckling to them. Move on, Mother.'

'*I* am leaving,' said Wilde, 'to dine with a new friend at Kettner's, in Church Street, is it not?'

'I know it well, sir,' came the kiosk boy's voice.

'I shall arrive at nine. Hurry, please, driver.'

'I'll make th' ol' mare go!' cried the jarvey. As the cab drove off and the constable paced away down Northumberland Street, I longed to depart. But the woman lingered to converse with the kiosk boy, and although to listen consciously would be unworthy, I felt it would not be indiscreet so long as I made no special effort to overhear. I put my eye again to the knothole.

'Aaaaaaooooow! Another dynamite blast, I see. It's bad f'r my bus'ness. 'Ow's y'rs, luv?'

'Not so good, Emma.'

'It's 'ard, ain't it, makin' it honest. You're not goin' back t' it?'

'I'll do what I have to, like everyone else.'

'Like m'new boa? From a 'mirer in Whitechapel. Says 'e likes m'rosy cheeks. Oh, *no!*'

'Spreading the word on the Dilly, Charlie?' greeted the kiosk boy.

'Bringin' the good news t' the faithful,' said the man who had spoken to Holmes and me. 'Evenin', Emma.'

'Don't evenin' me! If you wasn't aroun', some of 'em 'd come t'me.'

'Not bloody likely. Our clients wouldn't be any 'appier with you than yours'd be with us. Plenty f'r both, so live an' let live.'

'Fine f'r you, wi' a sal'ry fr'm The Guv'nor. I have t' feed a family.'

'If you want t'breed 'em, you've got t' feed 'em. Better t'leave th' buns in th' oven.'

'That's what y'r kine thinks! I wouldn' trade my little 'uns f'r all y'r fancy clo's an' fine food. An' my little girl won't be bred an' trained f'r th' Life like I was.'

'How's business?' asked the kiosk boy.

'We'd make a bloomin' fortune if we didn' 'ave t'pay you-know-oo. Them as cries "Shame!" in publick is th' first t' 'ol out their 'an's f'r a tip. We've got a new show t'nite, stunners wi' long talents, if you catch my meanin'. Come by an' see 'em. An' good luck t'you, Emma.'

'Bad luck t'you an' y'r kine!' shouted the woman after him. 'I'm sorry, luv. It's so 'ard feedin' th' little 'uns. If only my 'usban' 'adn't died in th' Joint. Aaaaow, why're we talkin' so gloomy? Ta-ta, luv. Come see the kiddies when you've 'alf a mo.' The woman momentarily disappeared from my view. Then, one of the planks was pushed back and the odour of Patchouli assailed my nostrils. ''Ullo, luv! I thot I saw a 'at movin' back 'ere. Why don't y'come out? Buy me a gin an' it, I'll make y' 'appy.'

'Thank you, no.'

'Aaaaooow! Another'v 'em. This's my night, ain't it? Come roun' when y'r ready f'r it, ducky. Ta-ta.'

Before anything more could prevent, I escaped from the hoarding and flagged a cab. Never has the trip from

Trafalgar Square seemed so long, but my spirits rose as we turned into Baker Street, for I knew that Holmes would be waiting at home for me.

It was not until I turned from paying the cab and it had driven away that I saw, on the top step, the most forlorn spectacle imaginable: little Billy, with a face full of tears and news, clutching a crumpled newspaper.

'They've killed him, sir!' he sobbed.

'Who?' I enquired dumbly, my heart suddenly turning to lead.

'Mr Holmes, sir. He's dead!'

CHAPTER NINE

A Fortunate Hansom

I snatched the journal and devoured with horror the headline: SHERLOCK HOLMES SAVAGELY BEATEN: LIES NEAR DEATH AT CHARING CROSS HOSPITAL.

For the second time in my life the earth seemed to sway and the world blurred, but this time I did not faint. Seeing no cab at the rank, I struck out on foot along the route which my cab had traversed. It is two decades since I was captain of the rugger team for Blackheath, and seven years since Holmes and I coursed the ghostly hound, and I found to my dismay that my sedentary habits had left me scant of breath. Soon, I was forced to slow and then, warned by ominous chest pains, to stop, looking helplessly about. No cab had halted in response to my frantic waving, and I had no hope that the one approaching would. To my surprise, the doors flew back and a high-pitched voice enquired, 'May I be of assistance, Dr Watson?'

'Charing Cross Hospital! Matter of life or death!' I called up. Only when we were flying towards Charing

Cross did I recognise my benefactor. He was of the exquisite type, high-nosed and large-eyed, and as usual he reminded me of a slithery, venomous creature. He was Langdale Pike.

Ever since Holmes and Pike had been undergraduates at Cambridge, Pike had pursued an acting career under the name Brookfield, while making a four-figure income from paragraphs he contributed each week to the garbage papers. Holmes discreetly helped Pike to knowledge and on occasion was helped in turn. I disliked the man intensely for violating gentlemanly behaviour. Since publishing my first chronicles of Holmes's cases, I had rejected theatrical offers to represent us upon the stage. Imagine my outrage when Pike wrote an 'extravaganza' which caricatured us, with Pike playing Holmes.

'My dear Dr Watson,' he said in his languid, affected voice which barely escaped being effeminate, 'may I enquire what—?' Wordlessly, I passed him the journal. 'Dear me. The best-laid plans—of course, I mean Mr Holmes's. You must be devastated, being such an *intimate* friend.'

'What do you mean by that?'

'Only,' with a reptilian smile, 'that I'm sure you were happy to return to living with Sherlock, after your more conventional marriage.'

'My wife died, sir!' I replied, my voice breaking.

'Of all ghosts, the ghosts of our old loves are the worst. But I see a Nevill's ticket in your waistcoat pocket. Have you been disporting yourself at the bath? So cosy, isn't it, like the St James's bar.'

'What do you know of the St James's?' I demanded with alarm.

'Only,' with a giggling laugh, 'that it is so—*so*—'

'I haven't the foggiest idea what you mean.'

'I believe you don't—poor man.'

Over my head the trap popped up and the cheery face of our driver peered in. 'Charin' Cross, sir. Record time from Baker Street.'

'Keep the cab,' said Pike. 'I must see a friend in this neighbourhood, to tell him about Sherlock.' Emotions warred within me, but courtesy won out. With hurried thanks and an admonition to our driver to 'Wait! No matter how long!' I plunged through the hospital door. 'He's just out of surgery, sir, Room C-33. Wait, sir! You cannot! I shall call the Director!' I bounded across the beeswax-polished floor and up the stairs. At the door marked C-33, I summoned my courage and pushed it open.

How shall I ever forget the sight: a clustre of doctors hovering about the bed, and in their midst the drawn and white face of my friend, his head girt with crimson-patched bandages. 'You can't go in there!' came a voice behind me, and then, 'Why, it's Watson!'

'Stamford!' I exclaimed, recognising despite a formidable array of whiskers my former dresser at Barts. 'I didn't know you were here.'

'Director, as of last month. You're behind in your journals, old man.'

I apologised, concealing my irritation at the pompous manner, so different from the young chap I had known two decades before. 'You're welcome to stay,' he added with extravagant condescension, 'though we have it well in hand: contusions, possible concussion, some loss of blood, shock—the usual things one gets when beaten with bludgeons.'

From the bed came a low moan. 'He's repeating his name,' said a doctor.

I leaned over the bed. 'Holmes, it's I—Watson.'

I was rewarded with a faint smile of recognition. 'Home—take me home.'

'But, Holmes, you are in no condition to—'

'Home!' the imperious voice rang out, and to everyone's horror the gaunt figure struggled up to sitting position, sweeping away restraining hands. He looked at me beseechingly. 'Home!' All my medical instincts rebelled at the thought, but even in extremity Holmes's strong, masterful personality dominated.

'Impossible,' said Stamford. 'Our responsibility—'

'*I* shall take responsibility,' I heard myself say, as imperiously as Holmes. 'I am his medical adviser.'

'This is madness!' Stamford's whiskers quivered like a muskrat's, but my heart leapt as I realised we had won. 'Come to my office. There are some forms to be signed.'

'Some' was a gross understatement I concluded, when he handed me still another and announced smugly, 'My own devising, based upon my observation of Dr Mortimer's mis-management when he was house-surgeon. It allows me to exercise absolute control.' Not daring to comment, I forged through the remaining documents, ruefully reflecting upon the corruption that absolute power had wrought upon one who had seemed so full of potential for aiding humanity. The need for making a living forces us all to make terrible choices, and often to betray the best in us.

At the front door I found Holmes, tended by our cab driver, an enormous man with a florid face and heroic moustache which gave him the appearance of a benevolent sea-lion. 'Why didn' you tell me 'oo I was wytin' f'r?' he demanded. 'It's a great honour, meetin' you both. We've read all y'r stories in *The Stran*' me an' the Missus.'

'We must get Mr Holmes home immediately.'

'O' course, sir,' he said, touching his forelock in the manner of his kind. With a tenderness which one could hardly have expected from his appearance, he picked up Holmes as if he weighed a feather and carried him down the steps to the cab. 'I know th' address, sir, as well as m'own.' While we re-traced our route, the door popped up over my head and, looking down from his perch on the dickey, he prattled:

'Fine ve'ickles, these 'ansomes. "The Gondolas o' Lon'on", ol' Disraeli called 'em. I was in noblem'n's service b'fore—coachm'n. We c'm up to' Lon'on an' soon as I sees 'em I says, 'Arry (that's m'name, 'Arry Baskerville) this's the life f'r me. An' I never regretted. You'd be s'pris'd at th' int'rest'n folk I meet. Take Mr Pike. I meet all sorts through 'im. Las' week I druv 'im wi' a bloke looked like a stablem'n, wi' red wiskers an' bowed legs an' an 'alf-witted look. I drive reg'lar f'r some folk. Take Mr Oscar Wilde. T'day I took 'im t' the Café Royal t'ave lunch wi' a comely lad 'e sent me t' pick up in Brixton. Mr Wilde always talks. I tell the Missus if I c'd talk like Mr Wilde I'd sell the mare an' turn writer m'self. "You can't make a livin' that way," she says. "Keep on cabbin' it an' write in y'r spare time." She's a rum 'un, my Missus Beryl (she was Beryl Kornet b'fore we was married). "'Arry," she says, "you'd best watch out wi' y'r lit'rary pertensions or folk'll take you f'r one o' *them*." (You know sir, them wi' the limp wrists.) I says, "Do I look like one o' them willow-stalks? Sixteen stone in m' stockin' feet an' that's a *man*. O' course if you want more proof—!" Well, that was the end o' that!

'I mentioned t' Mr Wilde once th't I 'ad lit'rary aspersions an' 'e said 'e c'd tell fr'm my talk I 'ad a nat'ral ability t'express myself an' I sh'd put things on paper reg'lar. I asks 'im if that's the way 'e does an' 'e says 'e puts 'is genius into 'is life an' only 'is talent into 'is work, so 'e writes 'is plays while on vacation. I've jus' about finished my book *Twen'y Years a Lon'on Jarvey*. B'fore I sen' it t' St Michael's Press, p'r'aps you'd give me some 'elpful 'ints, though frankly I don't see 'ow it c'd be improved. O' course there's no tellin' what the bleedin' critics'll say.

Sometimes I won'er if we read the same books, there don't seem to be any simularity in what we sees. But I s'pose they've trained their eye t' their trade, like Mr 'Olmes. "You see but you don't observe," 'es always sayin' in y'r stories. Sometimes I won'r wat I miss seein' in folk, like that red-'eaded bloke wi' Mr Pike.

'We're almost t'Mrs 'Udson's, sir, I c'n see y'r bow window, th'one th'air gun was fired through, as I 'eard Mr Pike tell some'un. I'll 'elp you up the stairs wi' Mr 'Olmes, seventeen steps t'Baker Street an' in this door. Lord, I feel like I've lived all m'own life in this 'ere abode o' noble bachelors. We'll jus' lay 'im on the bed 'ere. Will you look at those pi'tures o' celebrated crim'nals on the wall! That comely one mus' be John Clay, the forger. An' wasn't that stuffed snake skin we pass'd in the sittin' room the Speckled Ban'? (D'you think Dr Roylott really wanted t'keep 'is step-daughter 'ome f'r 'er in'eritance? You know what sycologist blokes'd say about 'im insertin' that snake through the slot between 'is bedroom an' 'is daughter's.)

'Yes, sir, I'll be glad t'step into the sittin' room. That's gen'rous o' you, sir, but there's somethin' that'd mean more than shillin's t' me. I've 'ere a copy o' *The Stran'* an' a bit o' pencil. Would you sign y'r name 'ere on the cover, it's not f'r me you un'erstan', it's f'r my wife. Yes, sir, I c'n see m'self out. One thing more, sir, if Mr 'Olmes'd jus' sign, too—o'course, I un'erstan', 'es too weak t'write jus' now. Yes, sir, I c'n let m'self out.

'P'raps I c'd come back another time an' get 'is signature. Would Mon'ay week be conven'ant? Thank you, sir. I know you mus' atten' t'Mr 'Olmes. I'll jus' be on my way so you c'n get back t'y'r resident patient.'

CHAPTER TEN

Wilde Revelations

With approach of dusk, Holmes's breathing became more regular, his heart-beat returned to normal, and he fell into a deep sleep. Several times I had caught myself dozing off, so I decided to ring Mrs Hudson for coffee to carry me through the night's vigil. As I closed the bedroom door, a long-faced Hopkins looked up from a chair by the fire. I slumped into another.

'Mrs Hudson let me in before she went to Mrs Turner's. Some of my colleagues at the Yard seemed glad to hear about Mr Holmes. They feel sore when he jumps in with methods they cannot use.' I nodded, reflecting bitterly upon the mole of human nature that prompts mediocrity to resent genius.

'It was fearfully close, but once the blood was cleared away the wounds didn't look so serious. We cannot know for sure until he wakes.'

'Wouldn't he be better in hospital?'

'He wouldn't stay. You know how masterful he is, even

when half-dead.' Hopkins winced, and I cursed myself. 'Besides, we can protect him better here.'

'In God's name, Dr Watson, what does it all mean?'

'It means murder, and I'm mortally sure they'll stick at nothing to get at him again.' I reached for the drawer in the side table and took out my old Adams six-shot revolver. 'I haven't used this since Afghanistan, but if anyone tries to enter this room—'

'Everything's moving too fast for me,' said Hopkins, his face a picture of bewilderment. 'First the Dynamiters, now this. But who—?' Quickly I detailed what we had heard from Lady Queensberry. He gave a low whistle. 'And you're sure it's Lord Queensberry who's behind it?'

'I shall go to the Yard and swear out a warrant.'

'Here, now, sir, the law requires evidence, and what have you got? Besides, he's a noble lord. You know how they protect each other. I'll wager even Lady Queensberry won't testify to what she said. Her duty to Mr Holmes ended with her warning.' My spirits sank again. What good for Holmes to regain his health, only to be struck down again by the same bullies? We both started as the downstairs bell clanged with a fearful noise. 'Billy has orders not to admit anyone,' Hopkins reassured me.

'Sir!' cried an alarmed voice below, 'you can't go up there!' I sprang to position next the door, revolver at the ready. Hopkins snatched up a stick and poised on the other side. Steps thudded in the passage and stopped at the door. Someone rattled the handle.

'I have a pistol!' I called out. 'Advance farther and I'll fire!'

We waited in silence for a minute—one of those minutes one can never forget. Then: 'You really must do something about this wallpaper.'

'What are you doing here?' I demanded, flinging open the door.

'There are paragraphs in all the late journals. I knew you would want me to come.' The presumptuousness was infuriating, but there was no denying his genuine concern. 'May I enquire—?'

'Two lacerated scalp wounds and considerable bruises. Morphine has been injected—'

Wilde's face brightened. 'Every misfortune has a silver lining.' With insolent self-assurance he lumbered in. I looked helplessly at an astonished Hopkins. 'I take it you expect some further threat,' said Wilde, turning aside my revolver barrel.

'I have sent for Holmes's auxiliary force of boys.' At the quickening interest in Wilde's face, I instantly regretted my revelation.

'I shall remain until their arrival. I congratulate you on your readiness and courage.'

I felt gratified myself that the old instincts, so well inculcated in Afghanistan, still served me well. 'I am an old campaigner. I didn't lose my nerve even when I saw my comrades hacked to pieces at Maiwand.'

'I've seen the monument to it in Reading; but didn't we lose the battle?'

'Not for lack of courage!' Memories of that fateful day—July 27, 1880—flooded back. 'When the Ghazis charged, our men stood steel true, blade straight. I was struck in the shoulder by a Jezail bullet and would have fallen into the hands of the murderous beggars if not for'—my throat tightened with emotion '—the devotion and courage of Private Murray, my faithful orderly. He threw me across a packhorse and brought me safely to the British lines. May God reward him, wherever he may be.' Without thinking, I took down the photo which stood upon the mantel.

'There is no memory so golden as one's war experience. I suppose the danger is part of its attractiveness. Who is the frightfully erect young officer by your side?'

'Captain Galbraith, the Colonel's son, killed in the volley that wounded me. We formed a friendship—'

'It often happens in the army or in prison.'

'You cannot understand! For a year of hard fighting we took the rough and the smooth together. He was my mate—and that means a lot in the army.'

'Who is the lad on your other side?'

'My orderly, Private Murray.'

'What an attractive boy.' I hastily replaced the photo on the mantel, not daring to look at Hopkins. Wilde picked up one of my mementoes. 'A bit of silver ore?'

'I practiced medicine in San Francisco, where my brother was dying.'

'I gave lectures there in '82,' offered Wilde. 'So infinitesimal is the knowledge of Art, west of the Rocky Mountains, that an art patron actually sued the railroad for damages, because his plaster cast of the Venus de Milo was delivered minus the arms. And what is more, he won his case!'

The laughter which rose in my throat stifled as I saw Hopkins's face freeze with horror. He was gazing at the bedroom door where stood Holmes, looking like some terrible ghost. 'Holmes! You should remain in bed!'

'Impossible. There is work to be done. Besides, Scotland Yard is lonely without me and it causes an unhealthy excitement among the criminal classes.' He advanced painfully into the room. 'The irony: struck down while only reconnoitring in Charles Second Street.'

'What did you see there?'

'What I expected to see. Sit down, Watson, you fidget me.' Holmes eased himself into his velvet-lined chair by the fireplace. 'This hurts my pride. It becomes a personal matter, and if God sends me health I shall set my hand upon these creatures.'

'This could have been a tragedy,' I said, 'if not for—who did you say came to your aid?'

'An ostler—some fellow with leather cords and gaiters. Came out of nowhere and pitched into those beauties like avenging fury. He must have been a fighter in better days. Took to his heels at the constables' whistles, but not before he said, "I wish you best of health, Mr Sherlock Holmes".'

'How did he know you?'

'A mystery. From his looks we don't move in the same social circles.'

'I shall enquire,' said Wilde. 'I haven't your distaste for the lower classes. Their prejudices are out of date, but there's much to be said for their principles.'

'It was Providence put that ostler there, Holmes, just as it gave me Private Murray at Maiwand.'

'Under the circumstances I hesitate to enquire,' said Wilde, 'but have you made any progress in the case?'

'I have made inquiries of Messenger-Manager Wilson. I helped him once.'

'Yes, I know,' said Wilde.

'Sidney Cartwright, who took Billy to the house, is brother to a boy who showed ability in the case of the ghostly hound. Wilson denies any knowledge of his whereabouts. The other boys believe that Cartwright recently came into money. I have engaged Shinwell Johnson, a reformed villain on ticket-of-leave from Parkhust, to search for the boy. When he is found, I shall quickly obtain details about Billy, and enough information about the notorious house to put a period to your friend's dilemma.' Holmes leaned back in attitude of satisfaction, and I could have cheered him.

'I suppose you regret now having proposed your preposterous competition,' I taunted Wilde.

'I am justly served for violating my own rule: Never try to beat another man at his own game—especially when it's afoot. My own research has not been entirely barren, however. Sidney Cartwright has been living in Brixton with a professional man, who was shocked when I told him at supper last night about Cartwright's activities. The boy has retired from the telegraph business on money paid him by a person of reptilian appearance, who implied that he was acting on behalf of a noble lord. Cartwright was to detain Billy as long as possible at the house, he told me.'

'He told you!' I ejaculated.

'During luncheon to-day at the Café Royal. Cartwright is an amiable lad, with one of those characteristic British faces that, once seen, are never remembered, and an uncultivated taste for fine food and wine. We are dining again next week.'

'Outrageous!'

'He was able to tell me little about The Private House—' I smiled in triumph '—except what he has seen, or has heard from other boys who go there to "work", if one may apply such a tedious term to such pleasant employment. The man who owns the house is in mid-thirties; his comely young associate calls him "Johnny"; everyone else calls him The Guv'nor. He has been in the Queen's service, possibly as a sailor. He once referred to the troopship *Orontes*.'

'The ship on which I returned from Afghanistan!'

'My throat is dry from so much talking. May I trouble you for a hock-and-seltzer?' At Holmes's nod, I tipped the gasogene and brewed the drink. Wilde raised his glass in toast: 'For England, home and beauty.'

'A traditional toast in the British Navy.'

'The British Navy has only two traditions: rum and

sodomy. Cartwright knows that The Guv'nor and Jackie have decoyed gentlemen—"so" and not "so"—to the house and, under compromising circumstances, demanded money with menaces. They also maintain The Private House as rendezvous for boys who are half men and men who are half boys.'

'Men!' I could not help remarking.

'The boys engaged there in the chase of the useful shilling are "so". Cartwright says they are treated well by The Guv'nor, who encourages them to save their earnings towards the day when their charms will have faded. Let me see, is that everything?' Wilde made a show of reflecting. 'The Guv'nor also acquires, from disaffected or greedy servants, incriminating letters which he offers to suppress or sell. There is a large, brass-bound safe in a curtained alcove of the downstairs drawing room. It has a triple-radiating disc lock. I'm afraid, Mr Holmes, that is all I have learned.'

I broke the awkward silence by remarking, 'I suppose Wilson was willing to put you on to Cartwright because he's one of your kind.'

'Messenger-Manager Wilson (who we thought was dead) is my half-brother, the result of a transgression of my father's that can seldom be attributed to those with my tendencies. Wilson is not "so"; he is the white sheep of the family.'

'I suppose we should be grateful to you for exploiting one of the perverted lads of this decadent metropolis.'

'The exploitation was mutual; my bill at the Café Royal was over a pound. And Cartwright is not a London-er. Most of these lads have come here from places such as Hampshire (where you were born, Dr Watson) and York-shire (where, I have heard, Mr Holmes was born). They were produced there by "normal" parents, and would not be here were it not for the cruelty which drove them to leave home and risk the hazards of a strange city. A few have vicious traits, such as a tendency to blackmail, but most are touchingly appreciative of any kindness, such as conversing with them as if they were of value. I am sure you would not be severe with Cartwright if you heard the tale of his early life; it was enough to sicken me with human nature. Now, Mr Holmes, what will you do with all this information you have acquired?'

Holmes had lain with his gaunt figure stretched out, his bandaged head sunk forward and resting upon his hands. When he lifted it, I saw that his cheeks were tinged with colour and his eyes almost as bright as before his injury. 'The art of the reasoner should be used rather for the sifting of details than for the acquiring of fresh evidence.'

'Quite.'

'I never allow cases to overlap. It is hard enough playing one game of cards; a double-handed one is quite impossible. But Billy's and your mysterious friend's cases must be connected. The thing is beyond coincidence. In Billy's case we must ask, why were such pains taken to lure him there?'

'Perhaps to lure someone else there.'

'Exactly. Today's ambuscade may have been their original intention.' Holmes leaned back in his chair, placing his finger-tips together and closing his eyes as he reflected: 'There is a great driving-power at the back of both these mysteries. I believe it is The Guv'nor of The Private House who is lending his services to the Marquess for a plot against me, as well as threatening your friend. When you have eliminated the impossible, whatever remains, however improbable, must be the truth. My apologies, Watson.'

'I can always believe the impossible,' said Wilde, 'but I can never believe the improbable. Cartwright told me that

The Guv'nor was provoked with him for bringing Billy, and has banned Cartwright from the house. You're out about this; your theory is too improbable.'

'It is improbable as I stated it, and therefore I must have stated it wrong. But my instinct felt the presence of the safe. It is necessary for the activity being carried on. Fortunately, the opening of safes is a particular hobby of mine.'

'How would you do that? With nitroglycerine?' asked Hopkins.

'Much too noisy, inconceivably messy, and quite unnecessary. A dial lock is nothing but an elementary exercise in mathematics.'

'You are the foremost in your profession, Holmes,' I said.

'And you,' said Wilde, 'are the best of disciples. You stand behind the throne and whisper that he is, after all, immortal. But Mr Holmes, isn't taking and carrying away illegal?'

'It is morally justified so long as our object is to take no articles save those which are used for illegal purposes.'

'I see that law, like virtue, has its degrees.'

'It's a mercy that you are on the side of the Force, Mr Holmes, and not against it,' said Hopkins.

'And a pity, Mr Holmes, that you are not in charge of the railroads: You would make them run on schedule.'

'Will you pursue this plan, Holmes, when you are well?'

He nodded. 'They are not yet ready to make their move, or we should have learned it from the agony-columns. What journals have you there?' he demanded of Wilde.

'The last editions. Would you like to read of your attack?'

'The agony-columns are particularly instructive. Pray give them to me.'

While Holmes perused them, Wilde and I leafed through the others. 'I really believe,' Wilde mused, 'that journalism justifies its existence by the great Darwinian principle of survival of the vulgarest. But at least we're not as bad off as America, where the President reigns for four years and journalism governs for ever and ever.' Ignoring his chatter, I searched the *Journal-Record*, discovering at the back a small item: INCIDENT IN KING CHARLES STREET:

> Late this afternoon, constables alerted by a red-whiskered passer-by discovered Mr Sherlock Holmes, 41, of 221B, Baker Street, lying unconscious in front of a residence in Charles II Street.
>
> Unidentified roughs, previously observed loitering in the vicinity, had beaten him with bludgeons. Holmes had apparently defended himself with his walking-stick, which was found broken beside him.
>
> The victim was taken to Charing Cross Hospital, where Chief of Hospital described his condition as 'guarded'.
>
> The owner of the residence expressed shock and outrage. 'This was done by a class of people who don't belong in our neighbourhood. We need more constables.'
>
> Sherlock Holmes, as all London knows, is a consulting detective whose occasional assistance to the municipal police has earned him the enmity of the criminal fraternity.
>
> We are sure that all Londoners join us in commending the prompt actions of the officers of the law, and in wishing Mr Holmes a speedy recovery.

I turned next to Mr Labouchere's tabloid, *Truth.* Its front page was dominated by an artist's rendering of Holmes, stick raised high, striking at a crew of roughly-dressed men. Above, was a huge black headline: SAVAGE ASSAULT SHATTERS PEACE OF KING CHARLES STREET!

Blood-curdling cries for help and the sick-ening thud of blows brought constables run-ning late this afternoon to a private house in Charles II Street. Mr Sherlock Holmes of Baker Street was found flailing with a walking-stick upon a group of men, who fled for their lives.

Details of the outrage are unclear, but a working-class passer-by volunteered opinion that Holmes had instigated the confrontation.

Public response in working-class neigh-bourhoods is running high at this unprovoked assault by a self-styled 'unofficial representative of the police force' whose exploits are puffed in *The Strand* by an ex-Army surgeon. Politi-cal groups representing the People have an-nounced their intention to march on Town Hall, demonstrate in front of Parliament, and shut down London Bridge.

By an irony that is its own indictment, Holmes, carried away with fury as he flailed with his stick upon the terrified victims, appar-ently struck himself upon the head, rendering himself unconscious.

He was taken to Charing Cross Hospital, where he is described as 'guarded', presumably to prevent his escape.

Mr Henry Labouchere, Liberal Member of Parliament for Northampton, champion of the working class and publisher of this journal, stated: 'It is infamous that the law allows this aristocrat-manqué to prey upon working-class people. I shall demand an impartial investigation to confirm his guilt and inflict appropriate punishment.'

Mr Labouchere concluded by quoting the motto of this journal: 'All we want is the Truth.'

The tabloid *Inquisitor* also sported a large headline: SUPERNATURAL PREDICTION PROVES EXISTENCE OF AFTER-LIFE!

The exact date, hour, and minute of the assault upon Sherlock Holmes was predicted a year ago!

Margerie Rogers, the well-known spirit medium, revealed today to *The Inquisitor* that the prophecy was made by the spirit of Edgar Allen Poe, who used the chimney as a speaking tube to say, 'It serves him right for aping Dupin!'

Poe enumerated seven coincidences between the fictional detective and Sherlock Holmes, and concluded by saying: 'If he really thinks Dupin was "a very inferior fellow", let him create his own character!'

Miss Rogers regretted that more might have been gleaned had not transmission been interrupted by the tintinnabulation of bells and the voice of a young girl, sobbing like the wind in the chimney.

Wilde, reading another journal, interrupted: 'Langdale Pike is still grubbing and grunting for pignuts in the bog of scandal. Only poets and scandalmongers know how useful passion is for publication. I suppose the public are pleased to find out other people's secrets because it distracts attention from their own.'

'Too late!' Holmes cried out, flinging down his journal. 'They have made their move, Watson. The letters will now pass out of the house.' He slumped, his face a picture of utter dejection.

I picked up the pages. 'But Holmes, this is a trifle.'

'You cannot conceive, either of you! It is not only our client who will suffer tragedy, but all of England!'

'The real tragedy,' said Wilde, 'is the Blackmailer's Charter, which degrades the law by subjecting it to cruel manipulation.'

Holmes lifted his head heroically. 'There is nothing more stimulating than a case where everything goes against you. We must on no account lose another instant.' He rose to his feet, his eyes shining and his cheek flushed with the exhilaration of the master workman who sees his work lie ready for him.

'Then may I remind you,' said Wilde, 'of the curious behaviour of my friend at the St James's Bar?'

'Your friend did nothing—'

'—to encourage the young man to approach him.'

'Who is this young man?' I enquired. 'And what is he to your friend?'

'Comely youths do not ordinarily invite mature gentlemen to their homes,' explained Wilde, 'unless they have a spurious "uncle" lying in wait.'

'Words, words!' exclaimed Holmes. 'Americans call it "the Badger Game". Many a man has been trapped by a scheming minx of a girl. You see, Mr Wilde, there are points of coincidence between your world and ours.'

'I have always suspected that,' said Wilde, 'but I never expected to hear it from your lips. What is this world coming to when we talk about our similarities instead of our differences?'

'As for your friend's secretary, who doesn't understand languages—'

'So that is why you spoke to him in German.'

'—and who is willing to work for half-wages—'

'Like half the women in London.'

'—if I could not put these clues together, it is high time that I disappeared into that little farm of my dreams and wrote my *Practical Handbook of Bee Culture, with Some Observations upon the Segregation of the Queen*.'

'How cruel.'

'Do I understand,' I ventured, 'that this secretary is—'

'—the young man from the St James's,' said Holmes.

'—and Jackie, accomplice of The Guv'nor,' concluded Wilde.

'How did you know?' I asked.

'Elementary, my dear Dr Watson,' replied Wilde. 'His eyelashes were too long.'

'But why would your friend employ him if he is corrupt?'

'To purchase his loyalty,' declared Holmes, 'and prevent his divulging the St James's incident.'

'I suspect my friend regards the lad as a victim himself,' said Wilde. 'He has done a stupid thing by employing him, but whenever a man does a stupid thing it is always from the noblest of motives.'

'Now,' said Holmes, rubbing his hands briskly together, 'we must use this time to apprehend Jackie and through him gain access to the letters.'

'My friend tells me the young man has disappeared.'

'I knew it when I read the advertisement. He has served his purpose.'

'How do you propose discovering him?'

'There are at least seven different ways, but time is of

the essence. Even as we speak the letters may be changing hands.'

My head was spinning. 'And to think, Holmes, all this came about because a man went to the St James's.' Holmes gave a low chuckle.

'Watson, you are not yourself luminous, but you are a conductor of light—bright enough to ensnare by.'

'You will set a trap for the young exquisite,' said Wilde.

'To beat him at his own game and the same place: the St James's.'

'How can you guess he will go there?'

'By putting myself in his place and thinking what I would do.'

'You have the air of a conjurer doing a trick. I suspect there is more to this than meets the eye. But ensnarement without warrant is illegal,' objected Wilde.

'Perhaps you would prefer to stand back from it,' warned Holmes.

Wilde rose. 'You are putting yourself in a false position. Morally, you are unjustified. And I deplore such action, especially against my own kind.'

'I understand. Would you care to leave?'

Wilde relapsed into his chair. 'How shall we do it!'

Holmes was quivering with eager activity, like a dashing foxhound. 'We shall personate one of your kind and draw this fellow's cover.'

'You may be discovered.'

'Watson and I have shared the same room for some years. It would be amusing if we ended by sharing the same cell.'

The idea of a cell had no attraction for me, and the thought of Holmes rising from his sick-bed to do battle had even less. 'I absolutely forbid it! Any exertion might cost you your life!'

'That is why I must beg your assistance,' replied Holmes smoothly. 'No one will suspect you, Watson. You are the man in the street.'

Wilde's face brightened. 'Where the best ones are found!'

'We shall also need one of the Baker Street Irregulars,' added Holmes.

'I have warned them for service.'

'The fair sex is your usual department, Watson, but as a writer you may profit from this. After all, "The proper study of mankind is"—'

'Men,' concluded Wilde.

'But I don't know anything about pursuing someone who is "so",' I objected.

'My dear Dr Watson," said Wilde, 'have you ever observed how a flower pursues a bee? You are still a fine specimen of manhood. You have only to go to the right place and be a good flower.'

'That, friend Watson, is the essence of the plot. What do you say?'

'I am here to be used.'

Wilde beamed. 'Mr Holmes, you have a treasure.'

'This is a serious matter!' I exclaimed.

'Nothing is serious these days, as witness Mr Holmes, who finds this only a pleasant opportunity to display his talents. While I *mot*, he reaps.'

The downstairs doorbell clanged. 'I suspect,' said Holmes, 'that is the Baker Street Division of the Detective Police Force.'

There was a pattering of many footsteps in the hall and on the stairs, and then entered, one by one, the youthful members of Holmes's small but efficient organisation, a dozen of the dirtiest and most ragged street arabs. As each marched the length of the room and came to rest drawn up in a row facing Holmes, Wilde appraised it with the eye of a broker. Last to appear was Wiggins, leader of the Irregulars, taller and older than the others. He froze in the doorway, staring incredulously at Wilde. I blushed that even this unsavoury ragamuffin would see us receiving one whose character was so obvious.

'Ten-*tion!*' Holmes barked like a drill-sergeant, and the boys sprang to attention.

'I see, Mr Holmes,' said Wilde, 'we do move in the same social circles: you for business, I for recreation.'

A piercing wail of expostulation and dismay, the voice of Mrs Hudson, as she ascended the stairs: 'I can't leave for an hour! This time he's gone too far!' She burst into the room. 'Mr Holmes, I am running a respectable house! What will the neighbours think of these disreputable little beggars coming here at all hours!'

'My sympathy, Mr Holmes,' said Wilde. 'I have had the same problem.'

Holmes addressed the boys: 'I have warned you before: Wiggins will come up alone and the rest of you must wait in the street. Now *march!*' All save Wiggins dashed for the door, dodging Mrs Hudson.

'And don't go sitting on my doorstep, either, or I'll call a constable! Really, Mr Holmes, this sort of thing must *cease!*' She marched out, slamming the door.

'Dear Mrs Grundy,' murmured Wilde. 'The only form of humour the middle-classes have been able to produce.'

'Wiggins,' said Holmes, 'I have a distasteful assignment for you. We mean to stake a trap for someone who is—'

'"So",' prompted Wilde.

The boy's apprehensive expression had turned to bewilderment. 'I think I take your meaning, sir.'

My loyal readers are aware that although Holmes's quicksilver mind worked in flashes of intuitive insight, mine is more accustomed to stolid thought and leisurely reasoning. A few times, however, I have been struck suddenly by a startling fact. This was one of those times, as the idle thought, Where have I heard that voice recently? resolved itself into the answer: The boy in the kiosk! My mind staggered. Although I was unconscious of any indiscretion, to admit having overheard the boy's conversations might raise unseemly suspicions in Holmes's mind.

'The poor lad is plainly frightened,' said Wilde. 'Wiggins, we know you are ignorant of the *odious* thing to which Mr Holmes refers. Have you ever known anyone who was "so"?'

'Not that I'm aware of, sir.'

'As with most people. Will you permit me to instruct the lad, Mr Holmes?'

'Pray continue,' said Holmes, observing Wiggins sharply.

'If Dr Watson will participate, he may gain practice,' suggested Wilde.

Reluctantly I came forward, drawn irresistably into a position I was helpless to avoid. 'I warn you, I sha'n't do anything unmanly.'

'We all have neglected opportunities to deplore,' said Wilde. 'Perhaps you will find it unexpectedly interesting.'

'How will I be dressed, sir?' asked Wiggins.

'Better than you are,' said Wilde. 'I dare say Mr Holmes has a fashionable costume for you, and I shouldn't be surprised if he lets you keep it.'

'Thank you, sir,' said the boy to Wilde.

'In addition to the money which he intends to give you.'

'I shall be very grateful, sir.'

'I shall expect you to be, by playing your part well,' replied Wilde.

'Yes, sir,' said the boy, with a sly smile.

'I sha'n't need make-up?' I enquired.

'All powder corrupts.'

'How shall I recognise those who are "so"?'

'If you have to ask, you will never know. If you were "so" you would recognise them by a tone of voice, by something in the eyes, by the way they move, and the way their clothes display their assets. Of course,' he added ruefully, 'sometimes one is misled by wishful thinking, and then *ghastly* things may happen. Now, you are waiting for someone to respond.'

'Will I have to wait long?'

'That is its greatest charm. As they say of torture, it helps pass an hour or two. Of course it is habit-forming, like drug-taking.'

'Get on with it,' said Holmes testily.

'Wiggins, you are standing casually at the bar. Can we provide Wiggins with a brandy? You like brandy, Wiggins.'

'In moderation, sir.'

'You shall have many. Now, the drama begins. There is nothing more fraught with it than encountering a new friend; there are always such splendid possibilities.'

'Should I encourage him?' I enquired.

'No, you are the object of this predatory boy's enlistment. Wiggins, advance upon your prey. Look him over. Radiate. Let him sense your Aura.'

It was only a charade, but as the lad advanced I felt intense prickling in my skin, as if every nerve were being tuned to concert pitch.

'You know he feels it,' Wilde encouraged. 'Now, a good first line is of the utmost importance.'

'Sir,' said Wiggins, 'do you have the correct time?'

'A masterstroke!' crowed Wilde.

'I see you have a natural bent for this, Wiggins,' said Holmes briskly, glancing at the mantel clock, 'but time is short and I must reduce you from principal to super-numerary.'

'Mr Holmes,' said Wilde, 'you have the air of an old hound who hears the view-halloa. I should like to see the end of this performance, but I have a subsequent engagement with my newest and dearest friend. We are now meeting at *eleven*.'

'We shall do our inadequate best without you,' said Holmes with asperity.

Billy entered. 'Sir, Mrs Hudson wants to know when you'll be pleased to dine.'

'Seven o'clock,' replied Holmes, 'to-morrow night!' He sprang to his feet, eyes shining with frenzied eagerness. 'The game is afoot! My nets are all in place about this man, and now the drag begins. By the Lord Harry, before this night is over he shall be in my power!'

'Bra-*vo!*' Wilde applauded limply. 'I have been called a shameless self-dramatiser, but I cannot hold a candle to your performance.'

'You intended to leave, did you not?' enquired Holmes icily.

Wilde collected his hat, cane, and gloves. 'I wish you all the best of fortune in your criminal endeavours: cracking a crib, misprison of felony, and ensnarement without warrant. I think you are all living wonderfully wicked lives.' He shambled towards the door. 'But beware. The Mad Marquess will surely come out on you again.'

'I have no apprehensiveness now. The only danger is the unknown. Once it is defined, it ceases to be a mystery.'

'I hate mysteries,' said Wilde. 'They are so obvious.'

'If you find my ostler friend, thank him for saving my life,' added Holmes.

'The heroic ostler. Not red-whiskered, I presume.' Wilde lurched out the door.

'Yes!' Holmes shouted after him to my astonishment. Wilde reappeared.

'Red whiskers? Stableman's gait and dress?'

'How did you know!'

Wilde lumbered back into the room. 'Bowed legs? Twitching hands? Hanging lower lip? Bestial and half-witted grin?'

'Yes! You know him!'

Wilde's face was grim as he removed his gloves. 'Some mysteries are not obvious at all. I wouldn't miss the wind-up of this one for the world.'

'If you know who it is, *speak*!' A dim, taunting image stirred in my memory. Where had *I* seen him?

'You were right, Mr Holmes. Your saviour has been a fighter: amateur light-weight champion of England. You owe your life to the most infamous brute in London: the Screaming, Scarlet Marquess—Queensberry!'

CHAPTER ELEVEN

Dragging the Net

*E*very head in the St James's Bar turned, later that evening, when Wiggins and I entered. I felt like a beetle under glass. Looking at the strange, fantastic poses of the clientele, their chins pointing up and heads thrown back, I marvelled at how different a thing appears when once your point of view has changed. 'Do you really think these are—?' I demanded of Wiggins.

'Some of 'em look suspicious to me,' he replied. One of the patrons smiled familiarly at him.

'Do you know that chap?' I enquired.

'Never saw him before. Shall I get you a drink, sir?'

'Whisky—double.' How I wished Holmes were here! Immediately after he had persuaded Wilde to depart, I had retired to my bedroom, my head in a whirl. Holmes had once told me, 'Among your many talents dissimulation finds no place.' Yet the entire burden of this adventure had fallen upon my shoulders, and I felt an ominous premonition that it would prove of fearful consequence to myself.

My experience of camp life in Afghanistan had made me a prompt and ready traveller, but this evening I had taken far longer than usual to dress, viewing myself in the mirror from one angle and then another. When I came downstairs, I found that Holmes had retired, apparently confident that Wiggins and I could carry out the meticulous plan which he had outlined. Now, Wiggins was engaged in conversation at the bar, and a middle-aged man with beard cut in Prince-of-Wales style was darting flirtatious glances at me. Despite my apprehensiveness, it occurred to me how helpful it would have been if women whose favours I had courted had been so open with their admiration.

'Do you see him yet?' I enquired of Wiggins. 'It's deuced uncomfortable, this waiting for someone to respond.'

'Those who are "so" enjoy doing it. Hard to believe, isn't it, sir?' Perspiration broke out upon my brow. Never, even in battle with the Ghazis charging and martini bullets flying about me, had I felt such cold fear clutching at my vitals. 'I'll recognise him from Mr Holmes's description,' added Wiggins. 'Pity you didn't see him at the hotel. What is it, sir?'

'Wilde was wrong!' I exclaimed, as two stunning women entered the bar on the arms of an escort. One, in green satin, was a tall brunette with a noble figure and demure and courtly air. The other, in red, had an olive complexion, large, dark eyes, and a wealth of dark hair.

'Sir, you don't want to have anything to do with them!' Wiggins's prejudice offended me. They were obviously not the sort that Society would regard highly, but I am an old campaigner, with experience of women extending over many nations and three continents, and my natural instincts urged me to show him how a healthy man behaves. 'Sir, you mustn't disturb Mr Holmes's plans!'

'Perhaps the game isn't coming. There's no reason to waste the evening.' The shy beauty in green touched her escort's arm and they strolled towards us. 'Leave me alone,' I whispered to Wiggins.

'I'm telling you, sir, it isn't a good idea!' Still protesting, Wiggins retreated, just as the fair charmer arrived at my elbow. Her hair was a rich hazel colour, and her cheeks were flushed with the exquisite bloom of the brunette. Although there was something subtly wrong with the face, some coarseness of expression, some hardness of eye, she was a striking sight.

'Thir,' said the escort, 'my friend believes she knows you.'

I laughed inwardly, drawing myself up to military erectness. 'I am Dr John Hamish Watson, late of Princess Charlotte of Wales' Royal Berkshire Regiment, 66th Foot.'

'Ee ees not zee man,' she said, adding with a coquettish smile, 'but ee ees very 'ansome.'

'Mademoiselle—may I—that is—enquire your name?'

She tossed her curls prettily. 'Violette du Bois.' Visions danced in my head of the Latin Quarter's easy passions. 'Eet ees zo tiring, standing, *n'est-ce pas?*'

'Would you care to—that is—sit?'

'Zank you,' she replied, dismissing her escort. I glanced about and noted with surprise Wiggins in earnest conversation with the bearded man. 'You 'ave been zee soldier?'

'In Afghanistan. At the Battle of Maiwand I was shot in the Jezail by a shoulder bullet.'

'I am an 'elpless woman, and I 'ave always depended on zee kindness of men.'

I took possession of her hand. Suddenly, I became

aware that someone seated on the other side of me had placed his hand upon my knee. A moment later, I felt the hand rise, and then a foot began moving slowly, insinuatingly, up and down my ankle. My fair charmer's eyes left mine.

'Zee gentleman beside you, ee ees a friend?' I glanced about, to see the bearded man. 'Ee seems very familiar wiz you. Oh! *Mon Dieu!* You are not—?'

'I assure you, I am a *man.*'

'*Pardonnez-moi.* Zay are zo strange, zee men in zis country.' What else she said I cannot relate, for my eye had been caught from the bar by the other charmer, who was darting signals no healthy male could mistake. My companion retrieved my attention. 'You find my friend attracteef?' I steeled myself for an outburst of feminine jealousy, but, astoundingly, my companion added, 'You would like to meet her, *non?*'

'*Non,*' I replied absently, 'that is, *yes.*'

'*Un moment.*' My charmer rose and went towards the bar. I knew I had only an instant.

'Sir!' I admonished the bearded man. 'We are not acquainted.'

'The hands,' he replied imperturbably, looking into the distance.

'I beg your pardon?'

'The feet,' he added, puffing on his cigar.

'Sir, I do not understand your—'

'The hands. The feet. Good heavens, man, have I taught you nothing?'

'Holmes!' it took all my self-control to avoid crying aloud.

'Speak as low as you can. I am here against my doctor's orders.'

'But what—?'

'You didn't think I would send you into danger alone,

did you, old man? But you disappoint me. The first quality
of a criminal investigator is to see through a disguise.'

'As your medical adviser I cannot permit you to—'

'The best medicine is the chase. You do remember
why you are here?'

'The quarry is nowhere in sight. You can't begrudge
me some satisfaction.'

'One of the most dangerous classes in the world is the
drifting and friendless woman. She is often the most
useful of mortals, but she is the inevitable inciter of crime
in others.'

'Holmes, I believe you are jealous.'

'You recall my methods: Never trust to general
impressions, but concentrate upon details. Have you
looked closely at your friend's hands?'

'Hands are the rule for men. With women it is the
sleeve.' The two women left the bar and advanced towards
us. 'I shall be pleased to serve you later, but for now allow
me to satisfy my natural instincts.'

Holmes snorted and rose from the divan. A moment
later a sweet voice said, 'My friend 'as found you very
attracteef, too.' I stood up to face the woman in red. She
was a perfect queenly figure, a little short and thick for
symmetry, but with wonderful eyes and a wealth of black
hair. She was a creature of the tropics, a child of the sun
and passion, who could be, I thought with a thrill, jealous
with all the strength of her fiery tropical love. My friend
said, 'Zis ees Dr John—'

'Jokanaan!' cried the woman in red, fire darting from
her eyes. 'All other men are hateful to me, but thou art
beautiful! I am athirst for thy body, Jokanaan!' She
reached towards me. Instinctively I retreated, falling back
upon the divan. She glided down beside me, entwining her
hands in my hair. 'It is of thy head I am enamoured,
Jokanaan. There is nothing so black as thy hair. Let me

touch thy hair!' She seized my hair in both hands and tugged until I cried out with pain. I cast a pleading glance in Holmes's direction, but he turned away in a marked manner. She pressed her body insistently against me, her face straining towards mine. 'It is thy mouth that I desire, Jokanaan! There is nothing so red as thy mouth. I will kiss thy mouth, Jokanaan!' She did, long and pneumatically. I fought free, gasping for breath, amidst the laughter of the patrons. 'You've got a live one, Sally!' called one. I tore myself from her embrace and retreated, panting, to Holmes's side.

'Thou would'st have none of me?' She flounced away, followed by her tittering friend.

'Well, Watson,' said Holmes, 'have you satisfied your natural instincts?'

'Damned unladylike,' I exclaimed, straightening my cravat and only desiring to flee.

'Perhaps you will listen now. You know my methods. Apply them. Have you ever seen such hands and feet as your lady friends have?'

'Now that you mention it—' I said, studying them.

'I believe I mentioned it previously.'

'—they are a bit large.'

'You are coming along wonderfully. Large for what?' I must have appeared comical, drawing my brows and pursing my lips, my eyes fixed upon the two women who were surrounded by admiring men, one of whom familiarly slapped the hindquarters of the woman in red. To my astonishment, she slapped back with greater force. For the second time that evening my mind was jolted. 'Holmes! You can't mean—?' As I stared in horror, the satin-gowned charmer who a moment before had fixed her mouth to mine hoisted her leg onto the rail in a distinctly masculine manner.

'This is the last straw! I shall leave this cesspool,

London. I shall go back to San Francisco, where men are *men*!'

'Well, Watson,' said Holmes, in a voice devoid of commiseration, 'a pretty hash you have made of this.' I cast my eyes downwards, shrinking like a frightened pup from the stroke. It never came. When I looked up, Holmes's nostrils were quivering, his eyes fixed upon a point behind me. 'Don't move, Watson,' he said in a low, thrilling voice. 'The game is afoot!' Wiggins joined us. 'You must draw him into our net. If I see danger, I'll intervene. Good hunting!'

I dared not glance towards the door, but Wiggins supplied his eyes. 'You're his game all right, sir. I'll order a drink and tell him you're looking for someone new tonight' (my manhood recoiled from the thought) 'and that you're generous to any boy that treats you right.'

I mopped my brow and reflected upon my position: On one side of the room stood Holmes, disguised as someone who was 'so'. On the other side was Wiggins, who was 'so' but had deceived us into thinking he was not, but who was now pretending to be. Next to Wiggins were two men pretending to be women, surrounded by others who were (so to speak) women pretending to be men. Thankfully, amidst all this confusion I, at least, knew who I was.

'Do you have a match, sir?' asked a voice by my side. There could be no doubt that it was the comely lad Holmes had described. Above a tall, starched collar I saw the blue eyes, the flaxen hair, the sensitive mouth and brash shyness. He was dressed in a manner that well displayed his assets, and he held a cigarette. My mind, as I admitted earlier, sometimes works slowly. I pulled out my watch and answered, 'A quarter to ten.'

He seated himself beside me. 'Do you come here often, sir?'

'Occasionally, with a friend.'

'I understand, sir. It is your night out alone. Not nearly so enjoyable, is it, coming alone? I usually attend concerts with my uncle, with whom I've been stopping since I came up from Sussex. He's not very understanding about some things, but he is away to-night. Not to mince words, sir—there's no purpose, is there, between those who understand each other *so*?—I would be pleased to invite you home.' My mouth suddenly went dry. The lad added, with a hint of impatience, 'If you would like. . . .' Still I could not speak. He rose. 'Of course, if you don't care to—'

'I . . . should be pleased,' I managed to say.

'The house is only a few blocks away. Shall we leave now and avoid the crush?'

Passing the bar, I noticed that my two charmers were engaged in furious discussion. The shy one in green was tugging at the arm of the other, who spat back, 'I won't go now! I'm having a marvellous time!'

'Come on! There's trouble! The manager's gone for a constable. I told you we shouldn't've come here.'

'I won't show off my new gown in the same old dens of iniquity. You can, if you want to. Common, that's what you are, common!'

The doorway was suddenly blocked by a constable.

'Vi and Sally! Didn't we warn you girls last time at the Alhambra? I arrest you in the Queen's name.' As we passed into the corridor, I was relieved to see that Holmes was following us at a discreet distance. 'Come along, dear, you know I don't like it, but I've got my job.'

'I didn't do anything! I was with this gentleman's friend!'

I glanced back. To my horror I saw Holmes, trapped in the doorway, clutched by the woman in green. 'Tell him we're together!' she pleaded.

'In that case, sir, I'll have to take you along, too. You can speak your piece at Bow Street.'

The boy was glaring at me with impatience. For an instant Holmes's eyes met mine and said: 'Go on! I'll get free and follow you somehow.'

With a heavy heart I followed the boy down the hall, pursued by a shrill voice crying: 'Take your hands off me! I am a queen and thou dost scorn me! *Bring me the head of Jokanaan!*'

CHAPTER TWELVE

The Tale of a Ghostly Hound

A grey curtain, broken only by the blurred haloes of the gas-lamps, had descended over London when the young man and I emerged from the St James's. A cab would have been useless, so we struck out on foot. As we walked the few blocks down Regent Street through the greasy swirl, figures so blurred and indistinct that I could scarcely tell whether they were men or women loomed up before us briefly, then blended into the cloud bank again, leaving me wondering whether they had only been ghosts of my imagination. In the distance, Big Ben began tolling ten, and my mind, oppressed with dark foreboding, recalled a phrase from a West-Country legend: 'The dark hours when the powers of evil are exalted.'

At the Raleigh Club we turned into Charles II Street, walking towards a two-storey corner building which was outlined by the yellow glare from its windows. Just before reaching it, we skirted a group of shabbily-dressed men smoking and laughing, and I glanced down a mews.

Suddenly there came back to my memory the Yew Alley, through which the ghostly hound had pursued the Baronet, innocent end of a procession of ancestors amongst whom lurked a dreadful tendency which came down to haunt him.

My heart pounded violently, my feet faltered upon the pavement, and for a moment I feared to continue. But the thought of Holmes, trapped at Bow Street Station and desperately trying to free himself, recalled me to duty, and I reminded myself that the ghostly hound had, after all, turned out to be only a human being, and one whom we knew at that.

In the entrance hall, faint strains of a music-hall ditty, 'Glycerina', hovered in the air, then faded as the drawing-room door closed behind us. The room was large and richly carpeted. By the dim glow of gas-lamps I caught sight of velvet chairs and a low-backed velvet sofa in front of a showy, white marble fireplace in which blazed a cheery fire. My eyes, however, were irresistably drawn to an alcove, partly covered with a thin curtain, behind which I knew reposed the brass-bound safe that was the object of Holmes's attentions. As soon as the young man excused himself to get the liquor-tray and the door closed behind him, I sprang forward and flung back the curtain.

The safe was precisely as Wilde had described it, with three concentric dials of numbers. I turned one tentatively, despairing that anyone could divine the combination that gave access to the pigeon-holes within. ('I am confident that I can have it open in minutes, if not in seconds,' Holmes had said, but that was when Holmes was free.)

Footsteps sounded in the hallway, and I scarcely had time to draw shut the curtain and pose myself leaning languidly against the mantelpiece before the young man entered.

'You're a doctor, aren't you, sir?' he remarked as he

poured my drink. My expressive face must have betrayed surprise. 'The nitrate stain on your finger. Doctors are always good-natured and uncommonly well-off, too. They don't mind paying for the good things in life.' He raised his glass. 'For England, home and beauty. That's my uncle's favourite toast.'

I was grateful for the drink, as the large fire made the room stifling. 'Why don't you remove your coat, sir?' urged the boy. 'It's quite proper; there's nobody here but us.' He was already undoing my waistcoat buttons, his nimble fingers darting over the pockets where I carried my pill-box and my watch. 'You must have a fine watch on that ribbon.'

'My father's, and then my elder brother's.'

'May I see it, sir?' A dim recollection of the masked man's narrative stirred in my mind, but I could not remember the next act in the drama. I was determined, however, to keep far from the young man, so while he turned the watch from side to side in the flickering firelight, I seated myself at some distance on the couch. 'H.W. Your father's initials?'

'Watson.'

'That's Scottish, isn't it?' My mind conjured up the faces of my unhappy older brother, whose hand I had clung to as a boy, and my ineffectual father, who had given him the watch on his deathbed. 'You have not taken care of it,' said the young man, gliding down onto the sofa beside me. 'It is dinted in two places, and the casing is cut and marked.' I moved farther towards the end of the couch. 'But of course, your brother had it.' Relentlessly, he slid along the cushions until he was once more in contact, and I realised with alarm that my back was against the arm-rest. 'Thank you for showing it to me,' he said, holding out the watch. My memory suddenly supplied the masked man's words: 'It slipped from our hands into his lap and thence to the cushion.' I withdrew my hand, but the young man thrust the watch at me and it fell into my own lap. I fought to rise, but he leaned against me, his head virtually in my lap, the weight of his body upon mine.

From behind us came the sound of a door opening and a hearty voice: 'Jackie, m'boy—what in the name of—?' I tore myself free from the young man's embrace and struggled to my feet, noting with dismay that my clothes were not only disheveled but open. I turned away, fumbling to close them. 'What are you forcing upon my nephew! This is police-court business!'

The young man leapt up from the floor where he had tumbled. 'Uncle—!'

'I understand, Jackie-boy. You see the sort of man I've warned you against. Will you face me, sir!' Steeling myself for confrontation, I turned about, to see a well-built man of middle years and military mien, with a straight, severe face, firm-set, thin-lipped mouth shaded by a moustache, and swarthy features convulsed with passion. At sight of my face, his eyes widened and the stern expression abruptly changed to gaping astonishment. 'Dr Watson—I presume?'

'You presume too much, sir!'

'Dr Watson—' he repeated wonderingly.

'Johnny!' cried the young man in a shrill, tyrannical voice. 'You're blowing the gaff!'

The man's astonished expression softened further into a smile. 'Leave us alone, there's a good lad.'

'I can see it's a wasted night for me!' The boy flounced out.

'Dr John Watson. This is a great moment.'

[Editor's note: From this point in the manuscript to page 132 of this edition, for a reason explained in

Sherlock Holmes's letter (Appendix) the paper and hand-writing are significantly different.]

'You still don't know me?' he remarked with a dry chuckle, savouring my confusion. 'Or are you reluctant to recognise a ghost from your past? I'll jog your memory.' He snapped to military attention and barked: 'Sir! Princess Charlotte of Wales' Royal Berkshire Regiment, 66th Foot—Private John Murray!'

It was my turn to stare, transfixed with uncontrollable astonishment. My mind removed the moustache, smoothed out the lines of fifteen years, and there was my courageous and devoted orderly. 'Murray!' I gasped. 'What are you doing—?'

'Here? I might ask the same of you, if I didn't know the answer. Some of us realise it early and some late. It's a pity to waste the early years, but the greatest waste is never to know. Here, you've overturned your drink.' He took the glass. 'Does it take you back? Fifteen years ago, and I'm pouring your whisky-pegs on the plains of Afghanistan.' He spoke in a boyish voice the well-remembered words: 'You did want a whisky, didn't you, sir?'

The years fell away. I, too, was young again, standing in my tent with my faithful orderly, who anticipated my every desire. 'How did you know?' I replied, in a youthful voice that startled my own ears.

'Intuition, sir,' he replied proudly, as of old. Years descended again, as a middle-aged pensioner and a villain seated themselves in the most nefarious house in London. 'Whoever would have guessed, fifteen years ago, that to-night we'd be sitting here like gentlemen together. A man must live for something, and I've lived to find you. But in my own house—!'

'Your own house,' I repeated dumbly. 'But how—?'

'It's a long story. I'm sure you wouldn't care to hear it.'

'I should be most interested,' I replied, eagerly seizing the opportunity to buy time for Holmes to extricate himself from police custody and accomplish his plan.

The Guv'nor raised his glass: 'For England, home and beauty. I never had a proper home, or any beauty. I wished many times I could have told you that. My father deserted us when I was young. It makes you feel a mite unwanted. My little sister and I took care of each other. Then my step-father came, and there wasn't any love lost for good reason: One day I caught him playing with my sister in a peculiar way. My mother wouldn't believe me, so I made sure he was never alone with her again. But one day I got caught myself, with a stableman who was "so".'

'He enlisted you!'

'Lord, no. I was enrolled at birth. I can't remember a time when I didn't find men attractive, older men like you. But you must have realised; your mind wasn't as pure as snow. I could tell when you chose me.' My mind filled with revulsion. If not for spoiling Holmes's game, I would have ended the conversation. 'He gave me what-for, my step-father, called me "little bugger" and whipped me. We were having a hard time then. I knew my mother's feelings because I was so close to her. (That's something they accuse us of as if it were a crime—I wonder how they feel about their own mothers.) Then one day a man from London came to town. He was dressed like a parson, but he had an evil air about him. I saw him in a pub with my step-father, head-to-head. Next day, when I came home, my step-father had a pocket full of tin and my sister was gone. He'd sold her, you see. I went wild and got beaten again—he had five stone over me and he didn't fight by Queensberry rules. Put me out of the house, but I didn't mind. I was coming to London to find her.

'The stories I'd heard about the wicked city were true.

My first day here a man picked me up and took me to a house in Cleveland Street. It was strange to be given money for something I enjoyed so much, and I went back often when I wasn't working as a messenger boy or looking for my sister. I found her finally, in one of those houses. I'd stand outside, watching the men go in. Society said they could do anything they wanted with her, so long as they did it discreetly. I imagined them, going home to their own families.

'To make a long story shorter, I saved my money and offered to buy her. She was getting old for them—almost eleven—and she was sick. You know what I mean, Doctor.

'I didn't have enough money for doctors or hospital, so she wasn't sick long. After that, I couldn't stay in London; her face got between me and my sleep. So I took the Queen's shilling, and that's how I turned up in the Regiment. Freshen your drink? I'll have another. Fancy, sitting here like gentlemen.'

I glanced at my watch and desperately prompted: 'You were a defiant lad.'

'I had a shield around myself. No one was going to get through and hurt me again. But I met you. You were everyone I wanted and had never had: father, brother, husband. And you were warm and kind, like a woman. I knew I wanted to be with you, and you must have seen something in me. We ate from the same dishes and slept in the same tent'—Good Lord! My mind reeled back to us side-by-side in the tent—'and I found my heart wasn't dead after all. I thought you must have feelings for me, too. I promised myself I'd be your faithful hound, like Captain Bruce's orderly.' My face must have betrayed surprise. 'You didn't know Captain Bruce was "so"? We orderlies knew. And General Gordon—'

'General Gordon!'

'He liked the Arab boys. And General Lord Kitchen-er—' My mind felt bludgeoned. Not Kitchener! 'I heard a year ago that he and Lord Queensberry's son, Bosie—'

'This is monstrous!' I cried, putting my hands to my ears.

'That's how I felt—monstrous I hadn't known, when I thought I was the only one, or if there were others they were just the dregs of society. Freshen your drink? You look as if you need it.'

'Please—continue,' I said, glancing again at my watch.

'I was jealous of all the time you spent with Captain Galbraith.'

'There was no braver man in the regiment!'

'A hard nail, with no feelings, so different from you. But you were his type and he was yours.' My mind rebelled, and minute-by-minute my concern for Holmes grew. 'Of course, it all ended with Maiwand. When the Ghazis came at us, I almost ran, but you stood there—steel true, blade straight—with your hand on my shoulder, saying: "Steady. Stand like a man." I didn't care if I died, so long as I did it by your side.' He paused, as if expecting me to say something.

'You were always a brave lad. You just didn't know it.'

By his face, it wasn't the reply he had hoped for. 'When you fell, I didn't stop to think, but slung you over the packhorse. I tried to follow you to hospital, but they ordered me back to the lines. Then the retreat to Candahar, and it was months before I could get leave and go to Peshawar. They said you'd been invalided back to England the day before.'

'On the *Orontes*.'

'I stayed there, pining like a hound at its master's grave. There was an officer one night. Maybe I was stupid, maybe I did it on purpose. I was arrested. Stowed in chokey. Discharged in disgrace and shipped back to

England on the next trip of the *Orontes*. When we landed at Portsmouth jetty I was delayed because I had to see a doctor—result of a Parthian shot. (You know what they say about the British Navy.) The doctor was a nice fellow, eager to talk about a book he was writing, but I was off to London. I tracked you to a private hotel in the Strand. That time I missed you by hours; they said you'd just moved out to diggings with another man.'

'What day would that have been?'

'The day after New Year's, '81.' It was true! That New Year's Day I had met Stamford at the Cri and mentioned that I was spending more money in hotel than I could afford. Within an hour he introduced me to Sherlock Holmes, and the next day we took possession of rooms in Baker Street. 'I've often thought how different it might have been for me if I'd found you. I thought it would be easy, finding a doctor in London, but I was never in luck's way. I was still young, though, so I went back to my old trade. Now I wasn't fresh from the country. I had come out into the world and learned things. I was a soldier, too, and that's attractive to many, so I never lacked for company. But there was never anyone who wanted me for more than a night. There was never anyone who would have nursed me for days as you did, when I had the fever.'

'It was my duty to take care of a sick soldier.'

'And risk contagion in your tent? I don't think so.'

'Stuff!' I exclaimed, remembering the writhing form on the cot, the beseeching eyes, the grateful smile as I bathed his body—Good Lord! Beads of perspiration broke out upon my brow as I recalled, while moving the sponge over his limbs—.

'Then of course came the Labouchere Amendment. (Even Liberals draw the line somewhere; usually it's at us.) Suddenly we were criminals, just for being ourselves, and the boat trains were filled with those who were "so". A noble lord asked me to go with him. For a year we travelled the Continent, the usual places for our kind: Florence, and Paris (where those like us wear the green carnation). He got tired of me as an affair, but I stayed as servant, to learn what could help me rise in the world. May I pour you another?' I stole another look at my watch. Surely Holmes must be clear of Bow Street by now, but why didn't he come? 'Nothing like the finer things in life, is there? It's one of the reasons the other kind hates us so. One of them asked me, "Do you really have more than we do?" and I answered, "Not more, just more often".' Murray returned with the glass. 'By '90 I was back in London—probably because the only thing better than leaving London is coming back to it. I wasn't young any more, and it wasn't so easy to find company—our kind craves youth as much as the other kind does. Luck finally came my way, though, and his name was Jackie. He'd just come up from Sussex, fleeing a hickory-type older brother who was constantly giving a vile meaning to "brotherly love". He was a stunner and London would've eaten him alive. It didn't take us long to figure we'd do fine together.

'Everything was changed by the Blackmailer's Charter. It was a crime now, and all we had to do was threaten: The Law was as dangerous to them as we were. There's enough in that safe now to keep Jackie and me comfortable for the rest of our days. We own this house (I named it The Private House, for sentimental reasons) and the one behind the mews. But what's important is, now you and I are together.' As he sat down beside me, my muscles tensed and my manhood rebelled at the thought that, in buying time for Holmes, I might have encouraged him. Like a man importuning a woman he said, 'If you only knew how often I've thought of this moment—John.' He placed his hand upon my knee.

I leapt to my feet, desperately calculating the steps to the door.

'Gentlemen do not say such things to other gentlemen!'

He rose and advanced upon me. 'It's a shame they don't, if that's how they feel.' He placed his hand upon my shoulder. I pulled away.

'If you touch me again, I shall defend myself!'

'Am I too old? Are you like the others, who come here looking for—'

'I am looking for nothing, least of all that. It is unmanly!'

'It wasn't unmanly of me, was it, when I risked my life to save yours? I'm sure you've told that story a thousand times.'

'I wish you had left me to die. I won't be obligated to such a *creature*!' As the ugly word crackled from my lips, he recoiled as from a whiplash. His lips quivered, and his eyes searched mine.

'Creature,' he breathed, turning away. 'That's plain English, all right. Let's think about that for a moment.' He wandered to the liquor-tray and poured a drink, his hands trembling. 'Perhaps I was too forward. I should have given you more time.' He tossed down the whisky. 'Perhaps, if we let it sit now, we could—another time.' Had he not been beyond the bounds of wholesome sympathy, as he was outside the pale of human kind, I might have pitied him, gazing at me like a wounded beast at the hunter.

'Stand aside!' I commanded. 'This is unlawful detention!'

He came forward, his hands groping for me. 'I was too forward—I realise it now.' He grasped at me, and his manly voice rose to boyish treble. 'Don't leave me again! Please, sir, I beg of you!' And then, the words I had feared most to hear: *'I love you!'*

I struck him. With a hideous howl of agony he rolled back, his hand pawing furiously at his cheek. Then he fell limp upon a chair.

The hall door flew open, to admit the man who had accosted Holmes and me. 'Somethin' wrong, Guv'nor?'

'No. Close the door, Charlie.' Desperately I appraised my chances of flinging myself through the window and escaping into the street. 'So that's the way of it,' said Murray finally. 'A man has to live for something—and I lived to find you.' He rose unsteadily and again made his way to the liquor-tray. 'I've had ups in my life and I've had downs, but I've learned not to cry over spilled milk.' With trembling hands he poured a straight whisky and tossed it down. 'But there's something on the cross. Why *did* you come here, and why are you playing Sister Anne at the window?'

[Editor's note: At this point in the manuscript, the original handwriting and foolscap paper resume.]

The Guv'nor's man entered again. 'Are they comin' f'r the letters, Guv?'

'You saw the advertisement. They must be moving on the old man.'

'Don't y'think they'd tell us first?'

'It's not my lookout. I don't like their politics, but their money's good.'

'Guv, Wiggins is outside with a toff.'

'Wiggins, out on the game again? I thought he was prospering in the newspaper business and working for— what does the toff look like?'

'Tall, thin, sharp face, penetratin' grey eyes. Friend o' this here chap.'

'Hold Wiggins. Send in the toff.' The Guv'nor's jaw set hard. With great deliberation he chose a cigar and lit it. Then, transfixing me with his eyes, as bright and keen as rapiers, he said: 'It was Judas, wasn't it, who proved it's only those we love who can betray us? If you're here as a spy, you may find it harder to get out than to get in.' The door swung open, and Sherlock Holmes entered with casual grace, dressed in his usual garb and style. 'Welcome, Mr Sherlock Holmes!' The door closed behind him, and latches slammed home.

'You have heard of me,' said Holmes pleasantly.

'Everyone has, but I didn't know you'd heard of us.'

'You understand that from this moment you are under arrest.'

'It is funny to see you trying to play a hand with no cards in it.'

'So you think,' said Holmes with a quiet confidence. His eyes roved the room, resting for an instant upon the curtained alcove.

'May I offer you a cigar? Whisky? Perhaps you, Watson.' Holmes's eyes sought mine. 'Mr Holmes, you know this gentleman with whom I have been conversing, pending your arrival.'

'He has been my intimate companion for fifteen years,' replied Holmes.

'Intimate companion for—' The Guv'nor broke off, a startled expression upon his face. My heart pounded. What came next was surprising. With an easy manner which matched my friend's, The Guv'nor said, 'Before you take me away in derbies, demonstrate your well-known deductive faculties.'

'I have no time for trifles.'

'Or perhaps accounts have been exaggerated. I've never read them; I have no interest in real-life crimes. Give me penny-dreadful fiction and characters truer to life than truth; I don't care if things are false, so long as they hold my interest. If you won't show me your powers, I shall show you mine. You have told me nothing, have you sir?' he said to me, like a spirit medium before the séance. 'Yet I'll warrant, Mr Holmes, I could tell you much. He's a gentleman of the medical type, but with the air of a military man. He has been in the tropics and has undergone hardship and sickness. He has been injured in a battle.' I listened aghast, aware of Holmes's astonishment and the re-appraising gaze he was directing towards the self-satisfied villain, who added, 'I could tell you more, but I won't reveal everything at once.'

Holmes's reply surprised me. 'Beyond the obvious facts that you have served in the Queen's army on the Indian continent as a non-combatant, I can deduce nothing.'

It was The Guv'nor's turn to appear surprised. 'I have heard of your tricks. Of course, you have obtained information elsewhere. I know of Cartwright's luncheon with Oscar Wilde. (If he were my client, I'd advise him to avoid panderers like Alfred Taylor.' The Guv'nor's voice took on a tone of self-mockery. 'Better to rely on me: dependable, well-protected, and with a heart of gold.) As for the Queen's service, I usually claim the navy but—Ah! Carrying my handkerchief in my sleeve, as Dr Watson still does. But the Indian—'

'I won't insult your intelligence by telling you how I read that, especially as you make no effort to conceal the tattoo above your left wrist. I have made a study of them and have even contributed to the literature. The design is of a devil-worshipping cult.'

'Perhaps that explains the near-fatal illness which accompanied it. I thought you had done something clever, but I see there is nothing after all. And my non-combatant status?'

'Holmes!' I interrupted. 'Your reputation will suffer if you are too candid with your methods.'

'Quite right. Shall we get down to business?' I was

reminded of a prize-fight, when combatants circle each other, searching for a flaw. 'You have conspired with the Marquess of Queensberry to interfere with my page-boy.'

'If that's your strongest card, I suggest you throw down your hand. Those with my tendencies may mingle naturally—you would say "unnaturally"—with noble lords; that's another reason why Society fears us. But you cannot believe I would bring your attention upon my house. As for interfering with children, I leave it to those with the opposite tendencies.'

To my surprise, Holmes nodded. 'I asked only to confirm my own conclusion.'

'In that case, I suggest we terminate this interview.'

'You have conspired to extort with menaces from an august person.'

'A more interesting accusation. Can you provide details?' With perfect composure The Guv'nor seated himself, back to Holmes, facing me, and lit a cigar. Gazing into my face he said, 'Tell me a story, Mr Holmes. My parents weren't disposed to humour such childish pleasures. But do not stop speaking.'

'It is your practice,' said Holmes, pacing behind The Guv'nor's back, 'to obtain letters which suggest that persons of means have violated the Criminal Law Amendment Act.' My eyes were irresistably drawn to Holmes as, still speaking, he sidled closer to the alcove. A dim realisation arose in my mind. I shifted my glance back to The Guv'nor, who was still staring into my face. 'You also lure to these premises men who will pay for freedom from discovery under that Act.' I felt the muscles of my jaw tighten as Holmes half opened the thin curtain and slipped behind. 'Your confederate brought my client here, placed him in a compromising position, and relieved him of his watch, from whose inscription you learned of his identity. Sensing opportunity for greater profit, you insinuated your friend into his household, filling a position which involved opening correspondence, thus gaining access to addresses. So much I know as a fact.'

Nothing disturbed The Guv'nor's composure. 'Continue, Mr Holmes.'

'Shortly after, you saw a more lucrative opportunity. Would it bore you to provide Watson with details, should he ever choose to record the case?'

'Jackie met some men at a bar. He has a taste for low company and too loose a tongue. They offered us a longer price for the letters. Continue.'

'Despite your deplorable character, you are still an Englishman.' To my inexpressible horror, The Guv'nor rose, circled his chair, and advanced towards the alcove. I struggled to cry out, but only a gasp emerged. 'I am willing to believe you had no idea of the fearful consequences.' The Guv'nor stretched out his hand to the curtain.

'Look out, Holmes!' I cried, too late. The Guv'nor flung back the curtain, revealing Holmes stooped over the dials.

'Why, Mr Holmes, whatever are you doing in the closet?'

Door bolts shot, and The Guv'nor's man plunged into the room. 'Guv! Fight in the street! Some bloke an' them loafers next door!'

'Stop it, before it attracts constables!' snapped The Guv'nor. Holmes emerged, looking as cool as ever. 'Do not look so hopeful, Mr Holmes. I frequently provide Scotland Yard with useful information, and they return the favour by not molesting us here.'

'Johnny!' The door burst open again, admitting the young man. 'He ran into the house when I opened the door! He's somewhere upstairs! And there're constables in the street!'

'Find him! Before they come in!' For the first time The Guv'nor's voice betrayed apprehensiveness.

'The game's up,' said Holmes in his masterful way. 'Throw down your hand. If the constables come in, you will soon be in custody.'

'And so will you, Mr Holmes. It will be a tasty tit-bit for the Press, especially if I testify that you often come here to indulge your depraved tastes. It couldn't have worked out better if planned.'

'Langdale Pike!' I ejaculated, everything suddenly coming clear.

'You know Langdale?' said The Guv'nor to Holmes. 'Then you must be the detective with the "obvious tendencies" about whom he's been teasing his readers. Ambitious Langdale. He'll seize any opportunity for advancement.'

'Holmes! How will it look!'

'Caesar's wife,' said The Guv'nor. 'But you knew the risk when you came here.'

'Watson was in danger.'

'And now *you* are in danger. I'm sure some at Scotland Yard will be eager to destroy you on grounds of Morality— a weapon people often use against those they personally dislike. And the public! They will pick you over like one monkey picking fleas off another. "Does Holmes prefer effete pleasures rather than manly recreations? Are young people ever seen entering his lodgings? Does he ever dress in women's costume?"' I started. 'I see I struck home on that. "Is he married?" "No." "Does he pursue female companionship?" "No." "With whom does he spend his time?" "A bachelor friend, with whom he lives." "Hah!"'

'See here!' I remonstrated.

'It isn't what you do in this world that counts, it's what people think you do. Imagine a prospective client wondering: "What if the criminal is 'so'? Would Holmes betray his own kind?" And what police officer would ride in a cab with you, for fear of a fate worse than death?'

Holmes seemed impressed. 'I am in your power.'

'At this moment you are in Society's power to crush you with the fate my kind knows so well: the discovery, the arrest, the honoured career ending in exposure and disgrace. You will be pulled into the pit where so many others have been pushed.'

Again The Guv'nor's man burst in: 'Dozens of constables! At the door!'

'I'm sorry, Watson,' said Holmes.

'He will never practise again. What patient would be examined by him? What parents would bring him their child? Pity you don't care more for him; we might work something out,' offered The Guv'nor.

'I am at your disposal,' said Holmes with dignity, 'for any arrangement to allow Watson's escape.'

'Holmes! I will not allow it! It is unmanly!'

'Unmanly,' repeated The Guv'nor. 'At last we cut to the bone.' He strode to the centre of the room and tore up a drugget of carpet. With it came a trap door. 'These stairs lead to our cellar, and a passage to a door on the mews. I don't think the constables will be there yet. Surprised, Dr Watson? There is always an escape route, isn't there? And a dark passage to freedom—or imprisonment.'

'Go, Watson,' commanded Holmes.

'You are coming, of course.'

'I must remain to hold him in play. Justice demands it.'

'I shall not go! I could never see my face in the mirror again!' I protested.

'What a pretty pair!' taunted The Guv'nor. 'I suppose you've never said a tender word to each other, lest you be thought "unmanly". But I have only been playing with you. It was cruel, but—' he turned to me '—others have played cruel games with me. Your life was not saved at Maiwand so you could throw it away in London. Go, both of you. I am not a good man, but I am a better one than you give me credit for being. I promise you, Mr Holmes, I shall not leave this room until I leave it in irons.'

'Johnny!' cried the young man. 'You don't know what you're doing! You'll rot in gaol! You'll eat stinking meat in kitchen grease! You'll pick oakum 'til your fingers bleed to the bone! They'll break your body and spirit 'til you come to death or madness! We can all escape!' From the direction of the hall came a sound of pounding on the front door.

The Guv'nor shook his head. 'This trap won't fool them long. Someone must lead them away.'

'Come with us, Johnny. Please!'

'It couldn't last forever, Jackie-boy. We must take what Fate sends.' The Guv'nor lit a cigar, gazing calmly towards the hallway, beyond which the pounding had been joined by a cacophony of whistles. 'I believe the constables are about to break down my front door.'

Holmes's eyes fixed upon The Guv'nor's with, I could almost swear, a trace of admiration. 'This is a very tangled skein.'

'You are looking for a difficult explanation, but the truth is very simple. Perhaps someone will explain it to you one day—or perhaps not.'

Pounding and whistling were joined by a rhythmic smashing sound. 'You may safely trust me, Mr Holmes,' added The Guv'nor matter-of-factly. 'I have a proven record for devotion and courage. I had the best of teachers.'

'Trust him, Holmes!' I cried. 'If not for yourself, for England!'

For a long moment Holmes stood gazing into The Guv'nor's face. Then, with sudden decision, he stepped into the trap and down the narrow stairs. I hastened after him. From above me came The Guv'nor's voice: 'Goodbye, John. Don't look back.'

Sounds of rhythmic smashing overhead punctuated a shrill, petulant voice: 'You're destroying yourself, and for what! If you think . . . think I'm staying . . . with . . . Ohhhh!' The last cry was uttered in tones of abject terror, and when the voice came again it was the pitiful, sobbing sound of a child in pain: 'Oh, Johnny! I'm so *afraid!*'

My mind supplied the image of The Guv'nor, erect and imperturbable. 'Steady,' came his voice. 'Stand like a man.'

Not-so-distant sounds of a door crashing to; feet thudding in the outer hall; violent rattling of a door. Holmes sprang up the stairs, seized the trap, and pulled it down into place, plunging us into darkness.

CHAPTER THIRTEEN

Weir, Not a Mews

Darkness. Such darkness as I had never experienced. My hands groped in the sudden gloom of the cellar. Suddenly, Holmes's cold, thin fingers stole into mine and gave a reassuring shake. Then, with that cat-like instinct which he possessed to such a remarkable degree, he led me swiftly through dark passages and up stairs to a doorway outlined by bars of moonlight. A thin band across his face showed me his grave expression, and the realisation came home to me that we could be in greater peril, for The Guv'nor might have sent us into the arms of constables. Now, we were like his kind: The Law was as dangerous to us as were the criminals.

With thumping heart I watched Holmes engineer his thumb under a bolt and open the door. 'Come, Watson,' he whispered. A half-moon bathed the mews in a soft, uncertain light and silvered the edges of the cloud-bank which hung low in the lane. No ambuscade awaited us. 'You have saved my life and character,' I whispered.

'Having first endangered them. Now we must find a cab. Everyone in the house will soon be out. A four-wheeler?' Holmes's last words were spoken in utter amaze. The door of a cab, parked at the closed end of the mews, began to open. 'Quick, Watson! Back against the wall!' We flattened our bodies against the brick. My heart pounded as the door opened further and a figure clumsily descended.

'Journeys end with lovers' meetings.' Wilde lit a cigarette as blithely as if he were in his club. 'I anticipated your need for transportation. You have kept me waiting for several hours.'

'We're not safe yet,' said Holmes briskly. 'They'll soon be guarding the street if they're not already. *Hssst!*' Holmes sprang back behind the cab, pulling Wilde and me with him. At the entrance to the mews, silhouetted against the street-lamp, appeared an ulster-clad figure. He surveyed the mews, then turned his back, blocking the exit.

'Too late!' I exclaimed, bitter disappointment quickening the pain in my chest. 'And we can't go back.'

'Then we must go forward,' said Wilde, 'after dealing with this person.'

Holmes had drawn from under his coat his shot-filled life-preserver. 'Remain here,' he commanded grimly.

Wilde shook his head. 'I have some proficiency in the sport of boxing, though I don't fight by Marquess of Queensberry: I give the other fellow a fair chance.' He lurched forward and tapped the figure's shoulder. 'How good to see you, my dear Mr Hopkins.'

'Mr Wilde! And Mr Holmes! Thank God you're safe! They think I'm guarding the mews.'

A strangled cry rang out. It was mine, uttered as I crumpled to my knees, chest enflamed with agonising pain. 'Watson!' Holmes flung himself down next to me, his arm supporting my head. Through my pain I saw something in his eyes nearer to tenderness than I had ever seen before.

'My medicine,' I gasped, fumbling in my waistcoat pocket, only to find nothing.

'Where is it? Quick, man, tell me if you love me!' cried Holmes.

'Behind—in the house,' I gasped between spasms of pain. Holmes sprang up and strode towards the door. 'No, Holmes, you'll forfeit all!'

I have heard how angels descend to give aid in time of peril. Now, a black-clad figure descended from the carriage. Through a mist of agonised tears I saw a brown-bearded face beneath a black vizard. 'I have my own,' said a melancholy voice. I felt a tablet pressed beneath my tongue, and a moment later the tormenting pain receded from my chest. The masked man tucked his pill-box in my pocket, a *beau geste*.

'Quickly, sir!' urged Hopkins, dancing back and forth frantically between the carriage and the wall. 'They'll be out any moment!' Hands lifted me to my feet. 'There cannot be more than seconds!'

Stumbling towards the carriage, spurred by excited voices and whistles from behind the door, I suddenly remembered: 'Holmes! The letters!'

'Hang the letters! Into the cab, sir, or we're all for it!' Hopkins placed his hand against my backside and thrust me in. The others clambered in beside me. 'I'll ride up top,' said Hopkins. 'If they see us, I'll say we're official.' He sprang to the driver's seat and—

I cannot say what happened next, for exhausted nature took refuge in its last storehouse of vitality and ease from pain. A dark curtain descended over my mind and, half in sleep and half in faint, I passed from consciousness.

CHAPTER FOURTEEN

Leaving the Friends Behind

When I drifted awake, our four-wheeler was careering through the fog-shrouded streets, Holmes was holding a brandy-flask to my lips, and Wilde was saying, 'I think we may all congratulate each other at escaping, though you cut it rather fine, Mr Holmes. I had my doubts when you charged into the jaws of death.'

'What a fine man Dr Watson must be,' said a melancholy voice, 'to inspire such loyalty and devotion. If I had had such a friend, my life might have taken a different course.'

'How are you, Watson?' asked Holmes.

'Better. But what a pity we didn't get the letters.'

'Please accept my thanks, nonetheless,' said the masked man, 'and tell me how I may compensate you.'

'My professional charges are on a fixed scale,' replied Holmes in his usual formula. 'I do not vary them, save when I remit them altogether, when my powers have proved fruitless. Take my card, so you may contact me direct another time.' As Holmes drew forth his bulky pocket-book, a packet of papers fell. Instinctively, I reached for them, but a sudden grip on my arm restrained me. Holmes's eyes danced with anticipation.

Mr Wilde's friend picked up the packet. Then his lip fell and his eyes protruded. 'My letters! You are a wizard!'

It was one of those moments for which my friend existed. 'Forgive me this meritricious finale. I can never resist a touch of the dramatic.'

'But Holmes,' I protested, 'you never ceased talking—'

'A trifling parlour-stunt. At University I used to amuse my fellow-students by doing mathematical problems in my head while carrying on a normal conversation. Nothing one learns in school is ever wasted.'

'It seems to me,' said the masked man, 'that all the detectives of fact and fancy would be children in your hands.'

'Lecoq would have taken a week,' agreed Holmes, 'although the combination was simple: 27–7–80.'

'July 27, 1880,' I heard myself say. 'The Battle of Maiwand.'

Holmes's grey eyes seemed bent upon penetrating my skull. 'I suppose that date has significance for him, too.'

'We are not home safe yet,' warned Wilde. 'The Guv'nor is in custody. Public opinion allows police more freedom in dealing with my kind, so they often bully and threaten until the accused informs on his accomplices or victims. Perjury is preferable to prison.'

'That is a risk we must accept,' said Holmes. 'We will know when he is brought to trial in a few weeks.'

'They will be torture for me,' said the masked man, 'but no more than all the days of my comfortless, meaningless existence. If only I could find some happiness—'

'We are not brought into this life to be happy,' Holmes reproved him, 'but to do our duty, and no duty devolves upon him who is incapable of fulfilling it. I know the air of London has been sweeter for my presence, and when my time comes I'll die easier for knowing I have not lived wholly in vain.'

'If only I could say the same,' said the masked man piteously. 'I have tried to help others by charity but . . .' his words concluded with a gesture of helplessness.

'Most people's gratitude,' agreed Wilde, 'is but the secret desire for greater benefits.'

'In that case,' said Holmes sharply, 'you had better reward only those who have already benefitted others.'

'Do you think there is any hope for me, Mr Holmes?'

'The past and the present are within the field of my inquiry, but what a man may do in the future is a hard question to answer. You have genius—and genius has an infinite capacity for causing pain.'

'You know me!'

'From the instant when we shook hands at the hotel.'

'I am haunted,' said the man in his melancholy voice, 'by a great fear: that when I die there shall be no kind hand of a friend or relative to close my eyes and whisper in my ear a gentle word of comfort. I shall wander the earth, a perturbed spirit—'

'Evil, indeed, is the man who has no one to mourn for him,' rebuked Holmes. 'But keep your hands off your life; it is not your own.'

'Down the long and silent street the dawn, with silver-sandalled feet, creeps like a frightened girl,' said Wilde, nodding towards the window, where the East had been gradually whitening.

'Our ways lie elsewhere,' said Holmes. 'All virtuous folk have been long in bed. Hopkins has brought us to the hotel, and here we shall part.'

'Mr Holmes, you have given me hope and strength,' said the masked man, 'and an idea of how I may redeem my life. I shall not disappoint you. Dr Watson, I know some day you'll want to tell this story. Just report me and my cause rightly, and I'll be satisfied. That's all I have to say.' He stepped out of the cab and glided towards the door of the hotel, his long black cloak billowing behind him.

'Thank you for an entertaining evening,' said Wilde, descending. 'And should we meet in public . . .' He tipped his hat.

'Wait!' I called out, not to Wilde but to his friend. Fumbling for the pill-box which he had placed in my pocket, I clambered out of the cab and hurried after him. 'Your pills!'

'I have an unlimited supply,' he called back. 'I shall send you some.'

As I retraced my steps to the cab, Hopkins leapt down from his perch beside the driver and Wilde leaned forward to whisper to him. Hopkins's eyes widened. Turning his back on Wilde he enquired, 'Everything all right, Mr Holmes?'

'As I always say, Hopkins, you are the best of the Professionals.'

'As you always say, sir, "It was nothing." I'll find my own cab home to Brixton.' He handed me up into the cab. 'I hope you're feeling better, sir.'

'You are looking unwell, Watson,' said Holmes, as we rolled away.

I turned to look back. Blurred and indistinct in the opalescent London reek, a hansom approached the hotel, obscuring Wilde and Hopkins from my view. When it drove off, they had both disappeared.

My thoughts were in turmoil from all the bewildering events of the last two days. But the most bewildering thing of all I knew I could never share with Holmes—the words that Wilde had whispered to Hopkins:

'Would you care to join me for supper again, Stanley?'

CHAPTER FIFTEEN

Coming Together

A dreary spring evening. All day the wind had screamed and the rain had beaten against the windows. As evening came on, thick fog rolled in down the lanes of dun-coloured houses, condensing in oily drops upon the window-panes. Our gas shone on china and metal with the remains of Holmes's favourite delicacies: cold woodcock and pâté de foie gras, complemented this night by an imperial Tokay, sent by young Von Bork in thanks for Holmes's having saved from assassination his uncle, Count Von und Zu Grafenstein.

Ordinarily, we would have chatted for an hour over cigars, but to-night we were both in a pensive mood and I sat brooding on one side of the fire while Holmes scraped away at his fiddle on the other. Abruptly, his voice severed my thoughts like a knife: 'It is an evening to reminisce about your army career.'

Accustomed as I was to Holmes's habit of answering my thoughts rather than my words, this intrusion into my most intimate reflexions was startling. Holmes gave the dry chuckle which was his nearest approach to a laugh. 'Your mind has often been elsewhere, since we wound up the Wilde adventure two weeks ago. Tonight you were sitting there with a vacant expression and your eyes fixed upon the spot where your portrait of General Gordon used to hang, until you took it down two weeks ago. You looked from that spot to the place on the mantel where your army photograph used to sit, until you—'

'I won't have you mucking about in my mind!' I exclaimed, with a violence that startled myself.

Holmes leaned back with a look of infinite languor, and for many moments neither of us spoke. Then, in casual tones: 'You have a grand gift for silence, Watson; it makes you quite invaluable as a companion.'

'You have never spoken of Wilde's case,' I offered.

'Nor have you asked me to.' He idly unfolded one of the evening journals.

'Is there anything interesting?' I enquired.

'A leading article on the strange and sudden cessation of dynamite outrages, the death of an industrial aristocrat, and the first night of a new comedy by Oscar Wilde: *The Importance of Being Earnest.*'

'I can't imagine his being earnest about anything. Have you heard from him?' I quickly added, as Holmes's hand hovered over the morocco case.

'Once a case is wound up, a client's inclination is to put it out of mind. As Mrs Hudson says—' Holmes assumed her voice: '"You can't change human nature".'

I chuckled at the impersonation, and Holmes's hand moved away from the case. '"You can't change human nature",' I repeated, imitating his imitation.

'My dear Mrs Hudson,' exclaimed Holmes in embarrassed tones, 'I didn't hear—'

'That is what you may expect to hear when I'm doing

my duty. He's here again!' She favoured us with her giant moth impersonation, somewhat inhibited by the lily clutched in her hand.

Holmes's manner changed instantly to eager interest. 'And your lily—?'

'I wouldn't leave it downstairs with him! He'd have his hands all over it!'

A slow and heavy step on the stairs, and a moment later the man himself appeared, in evening dress: coat with black velvet collar, white waistcoat with watch and large bunch of seals on a black moire ribbon, very pointed shoes, white gloves with black stitching, silk hat, Inverness cape, ivory-topped cane, and a white carnation buttonhole. A person unaware of his character might have said that he looked superb. 'My dear Mrs Hudson, may I offer my services for redecorating your hallway? Peacock feathers appliqué, as Whistler did with my ceiling?'

'Not bloody likely. Oh! See what you made me say! I shall be waiting downstairs, Mr Holmes, *if* you need me.'

'I couldn't find any deadly nightshade,' said Wilde to Holmes, 'but perhaps you will accept these as a token of my gratitude.' He drew from beneath his cape an enormous bouquet of poppies. 'The best gift is useful as well as decorative.' Holmes passed the bouquet to me without comment. 'Bosie and I are on our way to the first night of my new play. You've heard of it, of course; all London must be talking. The first act is ingenious; the second beautiful; the third abominably clever. It is wonderful; it is genius; you must go.'

'We never attend the theatre, but I'm sure it is amusing.'

'I write my plays to amuse myself. After that if people want to act in them I sometimes allow them to do so. I hold the future of the English stage in the hollow of my hand. Tonight I shall touch the moon.'

'I hope it will be a success.'

'The play is already a success; the only question is whether or not the first-night audience will be.' He seated himself across from Holmes and lit a cigarette. 'May I also look forward to reading *A Study in Scarlet Marquesses*, when your zealous historian lays out his foolscap?'

'I fear that Watson distorts so much as to create fiction.'

'To be suggestive for fiction is to be more important than a fact; the only real people are those who never existed. I'm sure someday, Dr Watson, someone will rewrite your stories from the standpoint of psychology and make an immense fortune. When I re-read them recently in Algiers I was struck by the profusion of attractive clients and criminals: "well-built, fresh-complexioned, smooth-skinned, bright-looking" men, with "chest and limbs of Hercules". If we believe your descriptions, Mr Holmes has apparently achieved the fantasy of my kind: constantly to be sought out by the handsomest of men, like Elijah being fed by the birds. I am thinking of trying my hand at the detective genre, something like "The Strange and Singular Adventure of the Comely Baker's Buns: An International Scandal Which Almost Cost Three Queens Their Reason". I would probably help myself from Poe and Gaboriau. True originality is to be found in the use of a model rather than in rejection of all models and masters; it is only the unimaginative who ever invent. But perhaps the world is not ready for a mingling of melodrama and epigram. Forgive my rattling on, but it is so exhausting not to talk.'

'I fear that Watson may never be able to add this to his collection.'

'Some facts may have to be suppressed, but that is usual when people write about my kind: They think their only duty to history is to rewrite it.'

'Your friend has written me the terms of his new will. Imaginative,' said Holmes.

'Do not underestimate him because he is a man of the world,' replied Wilde. 'He has also written poems and plays—melancholy ones. I have suggested he contribute to literature by encouraging other writers.'

'You have not heard from him recently?'

'We have been in Algiers during rehearsals.' Holmes picked up his pipe, casually folding over the journal. 'And how has all gone with you?' enquired Wilde.

'My life is spent in one long effort to escape life's commonplaces.'

'Tedious, isn't it, not being in pursuit of the object of one's desires,' said Wilde, lighting a cigarette. 'But you must be satisfied with our case—or rather cases.'

Holmes nodded. 'Different exiguous threads, leading up to the same tangle. I should have realised earlier that although they intersected at Charles Second Street they were not connected.' There was an awkward silence. Then, they both spoke at once: 'There are some points—'

'I beg your pardon,' said Wilde.

'What were you—?' enquired Holmes.

'I insist. You were about to say—?'

'Only that there are some trifling obscure points—'

'And several unclear details—'

'You are very welcome,' said Holmes, lighting his pipe, 'to put any questions to me now.'

'And I shall throw light on anything still dark to you,' replied Wilde.

'It was Billy's incident that threw me off at the start.'

'You assumed that only my kind could be guilty. How fortunate that Mr Hopkins deflected you from rushing to the house. There were undoubtedly witnesses and a camera nearby to record your being brought out by constables alerted by the Marquess. How sensational for

Pike's column! How disappointed the Mad Marquess, when events did not correspond to his wishes.'

'The physical attack upon me—'

'Was an excess of zeal by his hired bullies, which was why the Marquess came to your aid. He had a far more subtle fate than bruising in mind for you—Caesar's wife.'

'When I met your friend, I knew it was no normal blackmail—'

'You addressed him as "Doctor"—'

'To confirm my belief he was not. When we shook hands I knew—'

'How, Holmes?' I enquired.

'—and the clay on his shoes confirmed the identification,' concluded Holmes.

'A fresh illustration is not an explanation!' I rebuked.

'The advertisement,' said Wilde, 'warned that the letters would be passed.'

'Do you really think my function consists only in waiting about for something to happen in my favour? The agony-columns are my favourite cover for putting up a bird.'

'You placed the advertisement yourself!' exclaimed Wilde.

'The Press is a most valuable institution, if only you know how to use it.'

'How did you know *la belle garçon* would go to the St James's?'

'We are all creatures of habit,' answered Holmes.

'Two weeks ago you would have said "you". Dare I hope your point of view has changed?'

'One is always free to hope.'

'The entire charade at the St James's was fixed up for theatrical effect.'

'After my assault I had to work with the conditions given me.'

'As Goethe says, "The Master reveals himself best in working within limits".'

'I did not foresee a clinging Mary-Anne—' admitted Holmes.

'You were taken to Bow Street but gained your release—'

'—because Lestrade was on duty at the Yard. His eyebrows were a study.'

'People are so quick to jump to conclusions,' agreed Wilde. 'Wiggins, of course, alerted me the instant you were arrested.'

'He seems to be avoiding me of late.'

'A friend of his met a violent death in Whitechapel. She left several children, and Wiggins has accepted responsibility,' said Wilde.

'Wiggins, with a family?' exclaimed Holmes with amazement.

'Mr Hopkins deserves commendation, too,' added Wilde.

'Some day he will be Commissioner of Police; he is the best of the Professionals. I trust he quickly found a cab to Brixton. Isn't that where you found Cartwright living?' asked Holmes casually.

'Yes, with a professional man. But to continue: I collected my friend, knowing he would be invaluable if there were chaffering about terms.'

'You have shown ability in this matter,' said Holmes in a tone of grudging approval.

'I have experience in these matters; experience is the name we give to our mistakes. It was fortunate, that disturbance among the group of men loitering next door.'

'Stage-managed by Shinwell Johnson; he was the man who ran inside. Everyone in the street was an accomplice,

engaged for the evening. Lestrade was with the constables.'

'Age doth not wither nor custom stale your infinite
variety,' marvelled Wilde. 'You were never in danger at all!
You were merely playing with The Guv'nor and Jackie—a
delightful game of cat-and-mouse with nobody hurt except the mice. Mr Holmes, you are the model aristocrat.'

'My profession would be a drab and sordid one if I did
not sometimes set the scene so as to glorify the results.'

'I had seven different plans for extricating you—' said
Wilde.

'Never think that because you control your Art you
can control Life.'

'You found the papers—'

'Clearly marked and separate.'

'—and disposed of the others?' asked Wilde hopefully.

'I know my client is innocent; I have no knowledge of
the others. The safe was transferred to the Criminal
Investigation Department.'

'Pity,' said Wilde. 'They often show an unhealthy
interest in other people's affairs. I assume they picked the
lock?'

'They tried—they failed,' said Holmes, adding with
utmost casualness, 'They finally had to resort to nitroglycerine.' With spontaneous impulse Wilde and I broke
out clapping. A flush sprang to Holmes's pale cheeks, and
he bowed to us like a master dramatist.

'I see, Mr Holmes,' said Wilde approvingly, 'we both
enjoy the immediate applause. If the green-grocer had
such a thing as a laurel wreath, I should send round for it.
I am sorry about the other papers.'

'I do not make the law; I only enforce it,' said Holmes
bluntly.

'But the Labouchere Law is such a *bad* law—'

'It is every man's duty to see justice done.'

'Duty is what one expects from others,' said Wilde. 'It is not what one does oneself. Now I know why Reggie and Harry suddenly appeared in Algiers. Perpetual banishment: It is so Greek, isn't it? Each of us lives his own life and pays his own price for living it. The pity is when one has to pay such a long price for a single fault. How did you escape the house?'

'I feel free to divulge other facts but—' Holmes looked towards me '—we have our secrets, do we not, Watson?'

'One last question,' said Wilde. 'The notorious Guv'nor—?'

'—refused to testify against his clients and was given the most severe sentence.'

'Philosophy teaches us to bear with equanimity the misfortunes of our neighbours. "He is justly served with his own treachery". Who said that?'

'I believe it was a Melancholy Scandinavian,' replied Holmes.

'There is something infinitely mean, isn't there, about other people's tragedies?' mused Wilde. 'In America I was taken to see a prison: a strange amusement, but Americans are great hero-worshippers and always take their heroes from the criminal class. I would like to visit an English prison, but it is difficult to gain admittance unless one is of the lower classes. I take it The Guv'nor was?'

'When one tries to rise above one's station in life, one is liable to fall below it.'

'And if one doesn't fall,' observed Wilde, 'Society pushes one. Now, The Private House is dissolved, its unaccommodated boys turned into the street, and The Guv'nor—'

'Safely engulfed in prison,' concluded Holmes. 'It is curious, but I feel I have known him before.'

'You sound like two schoolboys,' I said, 'chortling over a prank.'

'So we do,' said Holmes.

'So we are,' said Wilde. 'But Mr Holmes, be honest with me. It was not reasoning which told you Jackie would return immediately to the St James's.'

'I admit only that my methods contain a mixture of reality and imagination.'

'What you choose to call "imagination" is what others call "instinct" or "intuition", and both are the essence of Art. You may as well cease wriggling and admit it: We are brothers under the skin.'

'See here!' I cried, leaping up. 'Now you've gone too far!'

'An imperfect analogy,' said Holmes. 'Danger is part of my trade.'

'And frequently of mine,' replied Wilde. 'The danger is half the excitement. We both have our quarry, and they are wonderful, aren't they, Mr Holmes? Think of it: the sport, the excitement! You know the feeling when you come upon the right scent—a kind of thrill in your nerves. And when you have pursued your quarry to bay and finally stand face-to-face with him, is it not like feasting with panthers?'

Holmes disdained reply, so I put a firm period to the discussion by saying 'All's well that ends well.'

'Nothing produces such an effect as a good platitude,' said Wilde, rising from his chair with the air of one about to deliver an encomium. 'Mr. Holmes, you could not imagine what fate the Mad Marquess could devise that would be worse than death. His plot was diabolical. He knew that you value nothing—not even your life—so much as reputation. He planned to destroy you with the Press, which can turn on you like a viper and strike with deadly force. Think of the Pressmen's loathsome joy, the delight they would have had in dragging you down! And the British public, which thinks it is being moral when it is only being Philistine, would have echoed their cry of "Morality!"—the holy cause for which men are always willing to sacrifice others. And why did the Marquess scheme to bring this upon you? "Thou shalt not rise above thy station in life." You broke that commandment twice— when you helped Lady Queensberry and when you frustrated his plan to punish you. I advise you to take great care of the Marquess.'

'He must also feel doubly provoked by you, for challenging his authority over his son and for helping me. Take your own advice.'

'I always pass on good advice. It is the only thing to do with it; it is never any use to oneself. But your intuition is correct. Bosie's cousin has discovered that the Marquess intends to disrupt my play tonight with a bouquet of carrots and turnips.'

'Carrots and turnips!' I exclaimed. 'Whatever can he have in mind?'

'It is too tedious, this insistence upon scandal. He has left at my club an insulting message: "To Oscar Wilde— posing as a Somdomite." It is something that no gentleman could tolerate and still hope to retain the regard of Society.'

'Is that so important?' scoffed Holmes.

'To be in Society is a bore, but to be out of it is a tragedy. I see no alternative but to prosecute. I have others to think of: my wife and our two boys. And there is Lady Queensberry. I owe it to them to take up the shield of British law and the sword of British justice.'

'When once the law is evoked, it cannot be stayed again.' warned Holmes. 'You know the risk you are running.'

'It is best not to know. It is only what we fear that happens to us.'

'What have you done to Langdale Pike?' demanded Holmes unexpectedly.

Wilde appeared puzzled. 'Nothing *to* him; a great deal *for* him. I have given him good parts in my plays and overlooked his caricaturing me in one of his.'

'Did it survive?'

'Only a few weeks.'

'Unlike your own,' said Holmes pointedly.

'He has a part in my play now at the Haymarket.'

'A small part?'

'He said he didn't care to learn many lines.'

'*Your* lines! Are you aware that the Marquess has hired two retired Bow Street Runners to gather evidence about you?' queried Holmes.

Wilde's startled face fought for composure. "How do you know?'

'Queensberry approached me first. He said as your friend I should have first refusal.'

'What unconscionable cheek!' I exclaimed.

'Pike has appointed himself aide to Queensberry in running you to ground,' announced Holmes. 'He has suborned a hansom driver into leading the agents to a house which you frequent in Chapel Street.'

'How absurd of Pike. But why?'

'He is ambitious to be Censor of Plays.'

'Who better than he to recognise the face of Caliban? But at this holy season of Easter we are supposed to forgive all our friends.'

'Gregson of Scotland Yard says that Queensberry's investigators have entered the house and seized letters enabling them to identify and locate young men with whom you have been familiar. Queensberry's solicitors have probably drawn up a Bill of Justification claiming that the Marquess has denounced you for the public good.' Holmes's voice rose to a pitch of urgency. 'Tear up the card!'

I was amazed by Holmes's intensity, but Wilde seemed unperturbed. 'My mother would not allow it. She would consider it dishonourable for an Irish gentleman. Besides, since my father's trial I have always wanted to be a leading figure in one.'

'No jury will give a verdict against a father who appears to be saving his son from an evil companionship,' warned Holmes. 'You should—'

'Do not tell me to leave the country. Socrates did not flee, even though Crito opened the door for him.'

'Socrates was *continent*!'

'I cannot help it. I cannot alter it. Besides, Bosie says "We must destroy the brute." I have consulted a palmist and she assures me that I will win.'

'Do you believe in palmists?' asked Holmes derisively.

'Always, when they prophesy nice things.'

'When do they anything else? Do you recall a king who enquired of an oracle what would be the result if he made war against his neighbour? The oracle replied, "You will destroy a great nation." He did—his own.'

A knock on the door and Billy entered. 'Mr Wilde, there is a young lord below in a cab. He says you must come at once.'

'Tell the young lord I shall be down directly. And suppose, Mr Holmes, the king had no choice.' Wilde placed his hand upon Holmes's instrument. 'We are all violins; events play upon us.' Holmes slumped into a chair, his face a picture of exasperation. 'Besides, I have no fear. The working classes are with me—to a boy.'

'You are a wilful and foolish man!' Holmes fairly exploded.

'Whom do I wrong?'

'Yourself! All you do with your vaunted individualism is to dissipate your talents in self-indulgence—'

'*You* speak to *me* of self-indulgence!' Wilde's eyes blazed with uncustomary fire. He seized up Holmes's morocco case and flourished it. 'What right have *you*, for a mere passing pleasure, to risk those great powers with which *you* have been endowed?' He slammed the case triumphantly down. 'And what right has this man Queensberry to dictate to me! I cannot imagine what he wants.'

'His *son*!' Holmes's words resounded like pistol shots.

'You presume too much upon our lack of friendship,' replied Wilde in tones of offended dignity. 'You are a fixed point in a changing world, and fixed points have a way of being left behind when the world moves forward. You are the defender and preserver of a society that glorifies Order at the price of freedom, and hypocrisy at the price of realism, and regards as a settled part of nature that there should be one law for the rich and another for the poor. Am I the only person who has ever urged you to question the social values which you labour to preserve? He is the Philistine who upholds and aids the heavy, blind, mechanical forces of Society. I regret that I helped you against the Dynamiters. At least they are trying to change Society.'

'I wonder how Mrs Turner's husband would feel about your sympathy,' Holmes shot back, 'or how you would fare in a society governed by Dynamiters.'

'The way of paradoxes is the way of Truth—to test Reality we must see it on the tight-rope. When I stood here two weeks ago, I thought the problem was yours: how to find a criminal. Now I know the problem was the criminal's: how to find you. He, with the instinct of that class born to lose, and you, informed with the majesty of Society, sought each other through London just as those of my kind seek each other, until your journeys ended in lovers

meeting.' Wilde shook his head sadly. 'You and Society—
how you persuade criminals to surrender to you, just as
you persuade everyone else to surrender their freedom
and commit that worst of all crimes—the crime of not
being themselves.'

'I will let posterity judge me on the basis of how I have
lived my life,' replied Holmes with dignity. 'As for freedom: The greatest freedom is to be guided and compelled
by one wiser than yourself.'

'I shudder to think what may happen, Mr Holmes, if
all the citizens of a modern nation ever adopt that
philosophy.'

'We hear far too much today about the rights of men
and far too little of their duties,' said Holmes. 'You believe
that freedom is the right to do whatever one wants to do; I
believe it is the right to do what one knows one *ought* to do.'

'A comfortable philosophy for a world always to be
1895. But there is a fresh wind blowing through our
society. It will be cold and bitter, and a great many like you
will wither before its blast. Yet a cleaner, stronger England
will lie in the sunshine when the storm has passed.'

Holmes's face was a study in resignation as he replied,
'There is no more to be said.'

Wilde picked up his hat and gloves. 'Pity. I cannot
believe we were meant to be only antagonists: We have so
many differences in common. You hate me with a necessary hate, and wherever there is hatred between two
people there is a bond or brotherhood of some kind. Can
you really be inaccessible to all ordinary emotions?'

'Whatever is emotional is opposed to that true, cold
reason which I place above all things.'

'Are you like all the others, tyrannised over by sound
English common sense—the inherited stupidity of the
race? I think it is something more.' Wilde shook his head
sadly. 'I suppose in years to come psychologists will

propound explanations of why you had to separate reason from emotion, then sacrifice all emotion. I think it is simply the same with you as with my kind: something known only to your creator—and perhaps not even to him.'

Holmes forbore to reply. Wilde's eyes searched his face. 'Is there a fear of love, Mr Holmes?'

Holmes's eyes kindled and a slight flush sprang into his thin cheeks. He leapt up and strode to the mantel, tugging at the bell-pull. In a voice of sincere though intrusive kindness Wilde enquired of Holmes's back: 'Have you never wanted to possess your soul? Have you never allowed your heart to overrule your head?'

I caught my breath. Never could I have imagined anyone asking such a question of Holmes. I waited, expectant as Wilde, for a reply. None came.

'Pity,' said Wilde finally. 'You might be a better man.'

'And you,' came Holmes's voice from the mantel, so coloured with suppressed agitation that I could not help but wonder at the reason for such iron control over himself, 'do you always affect such contempt for human nature?'

'My philosophy of life is: "When it comes to human nature, always expect the worst. You will seldom, if ever, be disappointed".'

'Pity. You might be a better man.'

'Perhaps. But we shall never know, shall we? Either of us.'

Billy entered again. 'Mr Wilde, the young lord is *very* insistent. He says if you don't come *now*, he will miss the first interval.'

'I shall be down instantly. Mr Holmes, may I again invite you to my play? I assure you, if I am present in the theatre, I shall not acknowledge our acquaintance.' (Was it my imagination, or did Holmes's back stiffen at these words?) 'Tomorrow I shall see my solicitor about an action for criminal libel.' (There was no doubt this time, Holmes stiffened.) 'I shall take up the swift and sharp sword of British justice, for the cause of human progress and individualism. Not to do so would doom future generations to cruel repression. "Repression". It is a word borrowed from the psychologists—and should be returned to them as soon as possible. I wish you a very good night.'

Holmes turned towards us. I searched his face for some indication of the strong emotion which had disturbed him. But his face was set in that inscrutable mask which he habitually presented to the world, and not even I could penetrate it. Holmes came forward to Wilde and stood facing him, hands plunged deep in his dressing-gown pockets. I gazed from one to the other, and it seemed to me a marvel that two such disparate creatures could exist at once in nature. The silence seemed eternal. Finally, Holmes spoke:

'Dr Watson and I shall be pleased to attend your play at our earliest opportunity. We shall expect you to make every effort to be present in the theatre. And we shall be mortally offended if you do *not* acknowledge our acquaintance—my dear Mr Wilde.'

My astonishment was as nothing compared to that which suffused the face of Wilde, quickly followed by a look of defiant suspicion, as at some subtle ridicule. Holmes withdrew from the pocket his hand, and extended it. Never have I seen such a succession of emotions sweep over a man's face as now over Wilde's: puzzlement, disbelief, astonishment, wonder. But there was nothing in Holmes's manner—steel true, blade straight—which implied anything but respect.

Wilde drew himself up with dignity and extended his hand to Holmes's. I watched with agonised fascination as the two hands clasped. Then, Wilde lumbered from the room.

Holmes stood at the bow window looking down into the street, whence arose a babble of voices: Wilde's, a vaguely masculine but shrewish one, and a third which boomed out: 'Right y'are, sir! I'll make th' ol' mare go!' A sound of horses' hooves, wheels rolling away, and presently the street was still again.

'Holmes—was that really necessary?'

'The sword of British justice is swift and sharp,' he replied in a strangely distant voice, still looking down into the street, 'but the hilt is crafted for an aristocratic hand.'

'I suppose you'll be calling upon Wilde now to help you in all your adventures.'

'No, the old hound's best,' he replied, turning towards me with an expression of amusement.

'He didn't seem concerned about his friend.'

'Mr Wilde's mysterious friend is dead,' said Holmes, matter-of-factly. 'A higher judge has taken the matter in hand.'

'Now I sha'n't get my medicine. He said he had an unlimited supply.'

Holmes tossed me a small package. 'Delivered while you were out.'

'I suppose I should read the obituary.'

'You will find articles on the front page—quite a bit of it.'

When I opened the newspaper, a face instantly caught my eye—a man in his sixties with familiar dark hair and full beard, and the most melancholy eyes I have ever seen. 'But Holmes! This is—!' He put a finger to his lips as Mrs Hudson entered.

'I think I'll just be nipping around to Mrs Turner's. Her husband's coming home from hospital tonight. Isn't it a blessing, sir, those dynamite blasts have stopped? Her Majesty's law did the trick: If they can't buy it, they can't blow it up.'

'What a blind beetle I have been!' I exclaimed as the door closed. 'There must be an immense fortune. I suppose the relatives will all squabble over it.'

'Not if his wishes are carried out,' said Holmes, nipping off a letter transfixed by a knife to the mantel. 'He has left the whole residue of his estate to form—' Holmes read from the letter ' "—a fund, the interest of which shall be distributed each year as a reward for the most original discoveries in science and achievements in literature." The money will be administered by his country's Academy of Sciences—provided, of course, no hint of scandal pertains to it.'

'Which it sha'n't now, thanks to you.'

'I should like to think so.' Holmes bent his eyes to the letter and read again: ' "I hope the next time my death is reported it will be with kinder words than the first; that I may finally have achieved my hopes of benefitting humanity more than I have harmed it; and that I may have earned from some kind lips the consoling words, 'Rest, perturbed spirit' ".' Holmes dropped the letter on the table beside me. 'The words are those of a Melancholy Scandinavian.'

'You knew all along!'

'From the moment that I shook hands with him and observed nitrate stains on his fingers, the mark of a doctor—or the inventor of explosives. The clay on his shoes was kieselgur, which transforms nitroglycerine into dynamite. And the Buckingham Palace Hotel—' Holmes's eyes twinkled '—contains the international headquarters of the firm which manufactures it. As you know, I have an intimate knowledge of London and a strangely retentive memory for trifles.'

'They both lied to us,' I said resentfully.

'Quite the contrary,' replied Holmes, collecting pillows from the sofa and chairs and dropping them in front of the fireplace. 'When others speak by the card, their lack of equivocation may undo us. Mr Wilde's friend was truthful when he claimed an unlimited supply of nitroglycerine. And Mr Wilde was truthful when he said—from the very beginning, you recall—that I was not far out when I called his mysterious friend "noble". Now, Watson, you will excuse me. . . .' Holmes's hand moved towards the morocco case upon the table.

'Holmes!' I implored, clapping my hand over his.

'Is there something you wish to tell me, Watson?' I gazed into his piercing grey eyes. 'Then I should like to be left alone.'

With despairing heart I made my way to the door, but I could not leave without casting back a reproving glance at the morocco case and demanding, '*Why*, Holmes?'

He lifted his hand from the table. It held his pipe. He lit it and, with a decisive gesture, pushed the morocco case away.

'To brood—' he replied, sinking down upon the divan of pillows and leaning back in a position of dreaming meditation.

I went out, gently closing the door, but not before hearing him add: '—on the singular inextricability of human vice—and virtue.'

Appendix

Letter dated 5 April, 1928, from Sherlock Holmes of Sussex Downs to Hon. Frederick Mackintosh, executor for the estate of the late John H. Watson, M.D.

Your telegram at the time of Watson's death arrived at one of the few times when I have been away from home. It was a painful blow, when I returned, to realise that I had been deprived of the opportunity to pay my last respects. In the month since his death I have been feeling uncharacteristically downcast. So many memories of my old friend and companion, when we were boys together (or so it seemed) in a time and place that seemed forever filled with promise and adventure. It has been twenty-five years since Watson and I turned the key for the last time in our door at Baker Street. Since then, I have not seen him for longer than brief visits (when he appeared the same blithe boy as ever), and during the last years of his illness I did not see him at all. Yet scarcely a day passed that I did not think of him.

He was on my mind today when your letter arrived with the manuscript found on his desk. Although there seemed to be two, they are clearly parts of the same chronicle. The longer portion was written many years ago (as you see from the bold and strong hand of Watson's vigourous years) and the shorter one quite recently (obviously, from the straggling and irregular characters of his last letters to me).

I read his account with interest, marvelling as always (though I had taken care never to reveal it) at Watson's ability to put into a connected narrative the most perplexing tangle of clues and events, and regretful (as always) at finding it afflicted with the usual fault. How often had I exhorted him that detection is, or ought to be, an exact science, and should be treated in the same cold and unemotional manner. 'Put the force of reason before the farce of personalities,' I told him. Here, I still find the delicate analytical details sicklied o'er with the coarse human characteristics of a popular tale. Yet, as I read this chronicle, the facts, which once seemed so important to me, paled next to the living personages which Watson so vividly portrays. 'It is always with the best of intentions that the worst work is done,' Mr Wilde once wrote, which inspires me with a taunting thought: Would it not be ironic if my immortality would rest not upon my methodically-written textbook but upon these trivial and sensationalised tales, dashed off by Watson's pen? If so, it will be good old Watson, after all, who will have the last laugh.

I do not know how familiar you are with the fate of this case's dramatis personae, so perhaps you would like to hear what I know. They are all dead now, with only two exceptions besides myself. Lady Queensberry, despite inconceivable ordeals, has survived to her eighties, as beautiful and gracious (I am told) as when I had the honour to know her. She will outlive us all and prove the adage that 'Those whom the gods love grow young.' Her son, Lord Alfred, is also alive, having served a sentence at Wormwood Scrubs prison for the same offense of which his father was found innocent. As fate would have it, Watson was serving there briefly, as prison doctor, and Lord Alfred has paid tribute in his autobiography to 'Dr Watson, kindest and most considerate of men, who always had a kind word for me and lent me books.'

Young Billy grew up to have a rare sense of humour, which he often demonstrated with his impersonation of Charles Chaplin. He had just launched himself upon an artistic career when the Great War broke out, and he chose to enlist with a friend, with whom he had conceived a David and Jonathan relationship. He was a talented lad, as proven by two presents which he sent me for my birthday: his design for a graceful and attractive school, and a water-colour of the ghostly hound in full pursuit, so realistic that it raises the hackles on my neck. His untimely death brought home to me the tragedy of his generation—perhaps of all generations—the tragedy of promise unfulfilled.

Wilde's son, Cyril, also died in the War, never having been allowed to see his father again. Wilde's wife died a year after his release from prison, her own death hastened by travelling from Genoa to Reading Gaol to inform him of his mother's passing. Lord Queensberry died in 1900, embittered by estrangement from his family and rejection by his class. 'He that troubleth his own house shall inherit the wind.'

Langdale Pike, who gave for Lord Queensberry a celebratory dinner, ended his days in 1913 with the comfort and respect of his office: Censor of Plays. His death followed by one year that of W. T. Stead, whose articles had inspired the Blackmailer's Charter. He went down with the *Titanic*. (Further details of these men may be found in *Thirty Years a London Jarvey*, by the popular Edwardian author, Sir Harry Baskerville.)

I presume you studied Wilde's trials in textbooks, so

you know that his suit against the Marquess was quickly dismissed and Wilde himself brought to bar. The text-books do not make clear how the fair play of British law was compromised by the Press, which immediately pronounced him guilty. (Wilde had always been severe towards them, so in this also he was hoist with his own petard.) Scarcely a man in London did not feel that the maximum sentence of two years' hard labour was justified. The dissenter was Henry Labouchere, who stated that he wished it had been seven. I recalled Wilde's remark about Liberals.

Upon release, Wilde wrote to the Press urging reforms in British prisons, particularly for child prisoners, who were treated inhumanely. He wrote: 'It is the lack of imagination in the Anglo-Saxon race which makes the race so stupidly, harshly cruel.' It echoed perfectly my own remark in *A Study in Scarlet*: 'Where there is no imagination there is no horror.' As Wilde once said, 'What is this world coming to when we talk about our similarities instead of our differences?'

At the time of Wilde's trial I was powerless to help him, but during his last three years, when he wandered the Continent, I was one of those who (anonymously, of course) contributed to a subscription for his support. His last play has taken its place in the Pantheon of immortal comedies, and as one of his biographers has written: 'The good he did lives after him . . . the evil is buried in his grave.' The words are, I fear, derivative.

By coincidence I discovered, from Commissioner of Police Stanley Hopkins, that The Guv'nor also served his sentence at Reading Gaol. I wonder if he ever knew that they had played parts in the same adventure. (The Guv'nor died there, defending his young friend from advances by another prisoner, who was not 'so'.)

Of the Mysterious Friend: His name, once a household word synonymous with destruction and terrible suffering, has acquired a happier connotation, partly due to my advice (given with so little thought of its beneficient consequences) and partly due to my influence with the Royal Family of Scandinavia, which enabled me to overcome objections which might have prevented the realisation of his wishes. (I note that Watson, with typical pawky humour, has touched obliquely on this in Chapter Four regarding Mrs Hudson, conferring on her a distinction later coveted by many.)

Regarding publication of this manuscript: The Twentieth Century must be almost gone before the world will be ready to receive it. Put it away in a safe place, attaching this letter as token of my approval for later publication. (Perhaps the proceeds can be given to the shelter for homeless boys which you and Watson founded.) I am returning it to you, the shorter portion (pages 124–132) inserted in Chapter Twelve. Why Watson chose to omit it originally is a mystery, but far less than why, in the last days of his life, he felt compelled to write it. Perhaps he felt he was revealing a secret to me. I had, of course, long ago deduced the facts, and knew what Watson was unwilling or unable to tell me (and I suspected that he knew I knew) yet he maintained to the end an obstinate silence which stood between us. I am capable of understanding, and I think in this respect I am a better man than Watson gave me credit for being. But each of us acts according to his lights, and to the many acts for which I am indebted to him I must add this last. May he have achieved the peaceful rest which he deserves.

Now, to your questions about myself. I am living on a small farm here on the Downs, five miles from Eastbourne in Sussex, and am in good health except for occasional attacks of rheumatism. I live the life of a hermit: a strange life for most people, who confuse being alone with being lonely, but it suits me, for I was never a sociable fellow and have never been happier than when I was alone and working on my own little methods of thought. (I must confess, it was always a burden to sustain the demands of Watson's friendship, and once when I quoted the Bard that 'man delights me not' he brushed it aside with 'nor woman neither.' My refusal to invite him here caused him no little pain, but I knew that in time he would accommodate to a life without me.)

I have given myself up entirely to that soothing life of nature for which I have so often yearned during the long years spent amid the gloom of London. I enjoy the exquisite air, I walk along the cliff path that leads to the beach, but mostly I work on my magnum opus, *The Whole Art of Detection*. In odd moments I am compiling a trifling tome which I hope will replace the superannuated handbook *Bees: The Feminin' Monarchi*.

Although I usually see no one except Mrs Hudson, I am occasionally interrupted, as I was yesterday by a young man on a bicycle who stopped to ask for water and directions to London. He carried an issue of *The Strand* with 'Shoscombe Old Place,' the last case that Watson published. Unaware of my identity, the young man revealed that he had conceived an intense interest in us. He spoke of us and our adventures as if he had been there with us, and in tones with which, I imagine, pilgrims once spoke of visiting Canterbury, he declared that he was on his way to London to visit 221B, Baker Street. As you may imagine, I was vastly amused to hear myself spoken of as one who had passed out of life and into literature.

I attempted to carry on a conversation with the young man, but could learn only that he was determined to become a consulting detective or, failing that, a jazz singer, whatever that may be. I sent him on his way with best wishes and a jar of honey, and as I watched him peddle away I thought of myself—can it be fifty years ago?—when I first came up to London to find or make my fortune.

Mrs Hudson was less indulgent with the lad's idealisation of the past. 'It's all right to visit,' she told him, 'but don't try to live there.' Perhaps you did not know that Mrs Hudson is my housekeeper here. Shortly after I left London I received a letter from her, telling me that her dear friend Mrs Turner had died and asking if she might follow me because she 'wasn't cut out to be a London landlady.' What this meant I learned in researching my magnum opus, when I found that she could supply all the facts of my published cases extempore. She had never questioned us, but had stood in the queue outside *The Strand* offices awaiting each issue. It is curious to imagine her poring over accounts of adventures which she had known only from the periphery, thinking as she read: 'So that's what was happening.' I regret that we did not provide her with details then, an action that would have required little effort had we thought of it.

Those who know Mrs Hudson only from Watson's occasional references would be surprised to meet her now. When she came here, she insisted that I call her Martha. I do not encourage such intimacies, but she was adamant: 'Mr Hudson has been dead these thirty years, but Martha is alive and kicking!' I humoured her, especially in late evening, after I had finished my day's labour and we sat on the Downs. Our conversation often turned to cases for which no explanation was ever forthcoming, and she urged me to provide details, interposing questions and suggestions so perceptive that I once remarked, 'You missed your calling, Martha; you should have been at Scotland Yard.' I expected, of course, that she would reply, 'Oh, no, that wouldn't've been proper,' but she only stared out to the Channel, her eyes alight with the gleam I have seen in the eyes of old hounds who hear the view-halloa and can follow the hunt only in their mind's eye.

To bring my story to a point: Not long afterwards, with the first gusts of that cold and bitter wind that would sweep across all of Europe, I was called upon to infiltrate the German intelligence system in England. I was no longer able to call upon my auxiliaries: Shinwell Johnson was too old for service, and Wiggins too preoccupied with his chain of kiosks. I considered insinuating into Von Bork's household Wiggins's adopted son, Randolph, but Von Bork had no need for a caretaker. I was at wits' end when one day Mrs Hudson remarked, 'I suppose he could use a housekeeper,' and recommended herself! In vain I pointed out that the *rôle* called for considerable ability at management. 'I was a London landlady for twenty years,' she said, 'running the house by myself, and *not* with the easiest of tenants.' I protested that it would require considerable skill at acting. She impersonated herself speaking to a tradesman: 'Why, sir, I sent around that payment days ago. You'll have it by tomorrow, and in the meantime would you just send me a brace of cold woodcock for Mr Holmes to serve to an illustrious client?' Finally, I warned her that it would involve considerable danger. 'Danger!' she exclaimed. 'I was three days in labour with Susan, Lord rest her soul. What do *men* know about *danger*!'

If you have read Watson's story 'His Last Bow' you know how a ruddy-faced, pleasant old lady in a country cap helped me to foil Von Bork. Her life and the fate of England hung in the balance a dozen times, but she carried out her *rôle* without a flaw, playing no little part in thwarting German intelligence and winning the war. I told her as much, after we had retired again to our quiet life on the Downs, and thinking to please her I added, 'Men have been named to the Honours List for less service to their country.' 'Stow your honours,' she said. 'I *did* it!' Woman's heart and mind are insoluble mysteries to the male.

Recently, she has become an ardent supporter of the Suffragettes. Yesterday she thrust in my face a journal quoting Sir Arthur Conan Doyle saying: 'A strong mind is as disagreeable in a domestic circle as a powerful singer in a small room.' Her face was livid as she proclaimed, 'If *I* were in his domestic circle *I*'d sing him some arias—*and* a double encore!' She advocates women for Parliament, and even says, 'Some day a woman will sit at 10, Downing Street.' Against such Liberal excess I have been adamant, refusing to give ground even when she invoked the names of Elizabeth and Victoria, until finally one day she said, with a wicked gleam, 'You're right, Mr Holmes. That's why there's only a King Bee.'

In my younger years I would not have tolerated this, but as years pass I find myself more prone to womanly emotions such as forbearance. I suppose, if this continues, some day she will wear a beard and I a bonnet, a prospect that tempts me of late to reflect more upon a problem furnished by Nature rather than those for which our artificial state of society is responsible.

The evenings are long here on the Downs, and become longer each year as my manuscript blurs earlier and I must stop. We dine early, Martha and I, then sit beside our cottage looking out across the southern slope of the Downs to the Channel. Often, as I sit pulling on my pipe, my mind turns with satisfaction to the successful cases of my career, the ones which began shrouded in mystery and ended in triumphant clarity. But more and more, as shadows lengthen and I feel myself drawing closer to that dark alley where all paths meet, my thoughts turn, in that perverse manner of the human mind, to another puzzle whose answer was so clear to me in my vigourous youth, but seems to become more uncertain as years pass: this puzzle of masculine and feminine.

It is most perplexing. It may even be—I am inclined to suspect—the Greatest Mystery of All.

Faithfully yours,
SHERLOCK HOLMES